U0126348

·豫莎劇·

約／束

（改編自莎士比亞《威尼斯商人》）

彭鏡禧
陳　芳　著

臺灣 學生書局 印行

國家圖書館出版品預行編目資料

約／束

彭鏡禧、陳芳著. – 初版. – 臺北市：臺灣學生，2009.11
面；公分
中英對照

ISBN 978-957-15-1479-6 (平裝)

854.5   98020520

約／束 （全一冊）

著　作　者：彭　　鏡　　禧　　、　　陳　　　　芳
出　版　者：臺　灣　學　生　書　局　有　限　公　司
發　行　人：楊　　　　　　雲　　　　　　龍
發　行　所：臺　灣　學　生　書　局　有　限　公　司
　　　　　　臺北市和平東路一段七十五巷十一號
　　　　　　郵　政　劃　撥　帳　號：00024668
　　　　　　電　話：(02)23928185
　　　　　　傳　眞：(02)23928105
　　　　　　E-mail：student.book@msa.hinet.net
　　　　　　http://www.studentbook.com.tw
本 書 局 登
記 證 字 號：行政院新聞局局版北市業字第玖捌壹號
印　刷　所：長　欣　印　刷　企　業　社
　　　　　　新北市中和區永和路三六三巷四二號
　　　　　　電　話：(02)22268853

定價：新臺幣二五○元

西　元　二　○　○　九　年　十　一　月　初　版
西　元　二　○　一　二　年　九　月　初　版　二　刷

85401　　　　有著作權‧侵害必究
ISBN 978-957-15-1479-6 (平裝)

《約／束》應邀於英國莎士比亞學會（BSA）第 4 屆雙年會
「在地／全球莎士比亞」（Local/Global Shakespeares）
國際研討會
由臺灣豫劇團演出精華版《折辯、判決》
時間：2009 年 9 月 11 日 20：00
地點：倫敦國王學院綠林劇場
（Greenwood Theatre, King's College London）

導演	呂柏伸
副導演	殷青群
夏洛	王海玲
匡先生（慕容天）	蕭揚玲
巴無忌	劉建華
安員外	朱海珊
明書（行雲）	謝文琪
瓜諾	胡昌民
鮑大人	殷青群
衙役	吳祐婷
大食人	楊啟青

《約／束》完整版由臺灣豫劇團首演
時間：2009 年 11 月 28 日 19:30
地點：臺灣臺北市城市舞臺

並應邀於美國莎士比亞學會（SAA）第 39 屆年會演出
時間：2011 年 4 月 7 日 20:00
地點：華盛頓州美景市

隨後於密西根大學（安娜堡）演出
時間：2011 年 4 月 12 日 19:00
地點：密西根大學孟德爾頌廳

於斯克蘭頓大學演出
時間：2011 年 4 月 15 日 19:30
地點：斯克蘭頓文化中心

導演	呂柏伸
副導演	殷青群
夏洛	王海玲
慕容天／匡先生	蕭揚玲
巴無忌	劉建華
安員外	朱海珊
行雲／明書	謝文琪
瓜諾	鄭曉巍

鮑大人	殷青群
雷公子	林永瑋
索公子	張志忠
老管家	連慧真
安泰	蕭雅珍
章成	伍阿春
音樂設計	耿玉卿
配器	張廷營
服裝設計	林恆正
燈光設計	JACK
舞台設計	陳 慧

莎戲曲《約／束》問世有感

楊世彭

　　彭鏡禧、陳芳兩位教授合編的「莎戲曲」劇本即將出版，要我寫篇序文，這是摯友吩咐下來義不容辭的任務。

　　彭鏡禧教授是台灣莎學界的泰斗級人物，他多年來在台大外文系及戲劇學系執教莎劇課程，受益的學子多不勝舉；陳芳教授是台灣中文系教育體制下培養出來最好的年輕戲曲學者之一，詩文兼擅，治學嚴謹。這次兩人合作《約／束》劇本的編寫，運用陳芳教授在詩詞方面的長才，根據鏡禧教授的譯文撰寫豫劇劇本戲詞，真可謂珠聯璧合、相得益彰。

　　《約／束》一劇將由台灣豫劇團在今年十一月底於台北市城市舞台隆重公演，其中兩場主戲〈折辯〉與〈判決〉，已在九月間應邀在倫敦國王學院的「在地／全球莎士比亞」（Local/Global Shakespeare）國際研討會上獻演，獲得眾多莎學專家的讚賞。這齣戲由呂柏伸老師執導，豫劇皇后王海玲女士主演大食人夏洛，我雖尚未有福觀賞，但基於呂老師的導演長才，王女士的精湛演技，相信此劇必有看頭，也期待在十一月底的首演時凝神細賞。

　　我跟莎劇《威尼斯商人》其實頗有淵源。看過歐美職業劇團近十個版本的演出不說，我自己曾在 1984 年中譯執導過這齣戲，合作的對象香港話劇團乃是該地最大的職業劇團，場合是一座新劇場的落成。1987 年夏天，我主持有年的科州莎翁戲劇節（Colorado Shakespeare Festival）慶祝三十週年，我又執導此劇的英文版本，邀來曾在英國皇家莎翁劇團擔任主角 28 年的名演員 Tony Church 先生主演猶太人夏洛。飾演威尼斯商人安東尼的也有來頭，乃密西根大學戲劇系的系主任，而科大戲劇系系主任則搭配小角，飾演夏洛的搭檔杜保，其他大小角色都由科州莎翁戲劇節的優秀演員充任。這個陣容，在我的導戲生涯裏算是難得的堅強。我既參與這一中一英的兩大製作，對於《威尼斯商人》這個劇本，自然有份特別的感情了。

《約／束》這個劇本乃是一個為戲曲演出撰寫的改編本。它刪去夏洛女兒與基督徒私奔的次要情節，也刪去劇中小丑父子逗笑的片段，專注劇中的主線情節與第一副線。前者講述貴公子巴薩紐想追求富家女波黠而囊中乏錢，經由好友安東尼的背書向夏洛借款，讓好友簽下一份「還不起就割一磅肉」的奇特條款。後者講述波黠由於亡父遺囑的規定，必須讓求婚者在金匣、銀匣、鉛匣中選擇其一，而巴薩紐最終選對鉛匣，獲得波黠的芳心。劇中的高潮法庭一場，主線副線合而為一，聰明的波黠擊敗狠毒的猶太人，讓安東尼免除割肉之災。劇中一枚定情戒指的失而復得，更是副線劇情的引伸，將劇情推向團圓結局。這個改編本的劇名，也正反映劇中兩大情節線的結合：一磅肉的條「約」，以及定情戒指的「束」縛；兩位作者對劇情的節刪及處理，可算合適而充滿機智。

戲曲版本的莎劇，最常見到的現象就是把莎劇原文的詩意沖淡，主要獨白及長篇對白由於遷就較短的唱詞，往往忽略某些內容，更遑論顧及莎翁辭藻的華美，意境的營造，意象的豐富了。在這方面，《約／束》雖也受到同樣的「約束」，很多地方就比同類改編本高明。由於鏡禧教授中英文的深厚造詣，陳芳教授在古典詩詞上的通透精熟，這齣戲的唱段有時雖也偏離了原文、刪簡了篇幅，但卻保留相當份量的莎劇精華。下面列舉的例子，乃貴公子巴薩紐在選擇鉛盒時的台詞，我引鏡禧教授的譯文：

> 看來外表最難顯示它的內在：
> 我們總是被裝飾的物品欺瞞。
> 法庭裡，敗壞墮落的抗辯，
> 只消用慈善優雅的言語調劑，
> 誰不能把邪惡遮掩？宗教上，
> 哪一樣重大過犯沒有假道學
> 引經據典加以祝福，予以支持，
> 用美麗的裝飾納垢藏污？
> 有哪個壞人會那麼老實，
> 不穿戴道貌岸然的服飾？
> 多少個懦夫，他們心虛得像
> 沙子堆成的階梯，嘴上卻留著
> 赫糾力士或戰神的鬍鬚。
> 剖開膛肚，他們的肝白得像奶，
> 這些人裝飾了威武的虯髯，
> 不過為了嚇唬別人。細看那美貌，
> 原來靠著依量計價的東西，

　　　　這就造成了自然界的一項奇蹟：
　　　　粉塗得越厚重，人變得越輕浮。
　　　　那蛇一般的金色卷髮也一樣，
　　　　在風中大膽的嬉戲調情，
　　　　好個金髮美人：卻每每是
　　　　來自另一個頭顱，原先的主人
　　　　是躺在墳墓裡的骷髏。
　　　　可見裝飾品只是欺騙的海岸，
　　　　誘人進入最危險的大海；是美麗的
　　　　圍巾，遮掩住黑妞；總之，
　　　　狡詐的時代用它以假亂真，
　　　　騙智者上當。因此你這耀眼的金，
　　　　麥達斯堅硬的食物，我才不要你呢。
　　　　也絕不要你，你這蒼白庸俗，眾人的
　　　　奴才。可是你，你這寒傖的鉛，
　　　　雖然並不討喜，反而令人畏懼，
　　　　你的黯淡感動了我，勝過巧語花言：
　　　　這就是我的選擇。只求天從人願！

　　　　　　　　　　　　　　　　　　　（3, 2, 73-107）

這段 35 行的台詞，在莎劇中算是難得地長，演出時也往往節刪其半，到了《約／束》裏卻變成另一個風貌：

　　　　巴公子（攤手，唱）：

誰不愛金銀珠寶光燦爛，

華彩錦繡日日鮮。

誰不愛佳餚盛饌酒滿盞，

高車駟馬美衣冠。

轉眼間煙消雲散成虛幻，

富貴榮華難上難。

人世真假莫能辨，

天花亂墜總欺瞞。

自古衙門好手段，

矯飾言語是非搬。

懦夫誇勇蘭陵現，

倒戈只在彈指間。

罪惡擅以德行掩，

道貌岸然實藏奸。

外是金玉內敗亂，

細推物理探本原。

我可得——小心謹慎選一選，

成敗全看這一關。

（第三場：〈定情〉）

這段 18 行的唱詞，表述了莎翁詩詞要意，但以戲曲通用的七字句形式填詞，也都叶韻，成了真正跨文化的創作。鏡禧教授也在本書中把它譯成英文，再跨回去，成為下面的形態：

Who loves not shining gold and brilliant gems,

Or splendid brocade fabric for his use?

Who loves not dainty dishes, cups of wine,

Or handsome chariots and gorgeous clothes?

In twinkling, oh, they melt into thin air;

Illusive are high ranks and wealth and fame.

So may the outward shows be least themselves:

The world is still deceived with ornament.

The court has long been known as such a place

Where perjury and falsehood do prevail.

Oft cowards brag of bravery unmatched,

Yet they surrender 'fore the battle's joined.

Oft vice assumes some mark of outward good,

And treachery is masked by sober brows.

Look into ornament and grossness see:

This law discover and then search for truth.

In choosing, I too careful cannot be;

On this depends my failure or success!

　　鏡禧教授的譯文，居然還保留不少莎劇「五步抑揚格」的形式。這種「莎劇改寫成豫劇又轉譯成英文」正是本書的特點，其實也是彭、陳兩位教授的「再度創作」，其中趣味，值得細細品嚐。

　　《約／束》這齣戲的宣傳定位是「豫莎劇」，而我這篇序言卻以「莎戲曲」稱之，其實略有「私心」。當初陳芳教授要我細讀二稿時，我的直覺反應是唱詞既然填得這樣好，何不在豫劇版公演結束後略加修改，讓京劇或其他戲曲劇種亦可搬演？這個「莎戲曲」的文題，正期望這個劇本在出版後還有後續生命，那就不枉兩位作者的心血結晶了。

2009 年秋，上海旅次

（本文作者為美國科羅拉多大學戲劇舞蹈系榮休教授，香港話劇團榮休藝術總監，美國科州莎翁戲劇節榮休藝術及行政總監。）

弁　言

　　莎士比亞（William Shakespeare, 1564-1616）在《威尼斯商人》（*The Merchant of Venice*）中，設計了好幾層複雜的「約束」關係。就表面上的情節而言，一是巴薩紐（Bassanio）向波點（Portia）求愛，受到女方父親遺命以金、銀、鉛三個匣子選婿的制約；二是猶太人夏洛（Shylock）和威尼斯商人（基督徒）安東尼（Antonio）訂定了一磅肉契約；三是波點因巴薩紐把定情戒指贈送「他人」而生氣，引出戒指風波。這些紛爭，都是因為不可思議的「約束」所造成的。

　　其實，「約」乃是維護人際關係穩定的重要工具；約的簽訂，目的在於保護雙方當事人。既然如此，約的另一面便是「束」：簽約雙方都必須受到某種束縛。這種弔詭關係形成了《約／束》這齣戲的結構大綱，而約束的漏洞或執行的困難，則鋪陳為本劇的故事情節——約束，難道真能約束？

　　本劇初稿曾與導演呂柏伸兄討論，另承楊世彭教授悉心指導，耿玉卿老師、羅懷臻兄也提供了寶貴的意見；道沄精心設計封面；楊世彭教授更在百忙中為本書作序；臺灣豫劇團慷慨提供劇照、曲譜。謹此致上最深厚的謝意。

目 錄

約／束

人物表

夏洛	大食富商，以放高利貸出名
慕容天	貝芒縣的富有淑媛
巴無忌	尼斯府家道中落的世家子弟
安員外	尼斯府一大戶
行雲	慕容天的貼身婢女
瓜諾	巴無忌的書僮
包大人	尼斯府的府尹
匡先生	貝大人的幕僚（慕容天改扮）
明書	匡先生的隨從（行雲改扮）
雷公子	安員外的朋友
索公子	安員外的朋友
老管家	慕容府邸的管家
安泰	安員外的僕從
章成	慕容府邸的僕從
專差	貝大人的信差

求親者若干人

婢女若干人

孩童若干人

路人若干人

衙役若干人

場　目

序　曲

（地點：貝芒縣‧慕容府邸廳堂）

（婢女若干人上，穿梭忙碌）

〔伴唱〕：世事荒謬說不盡，

　　　　　嚴父遺命定終身。

　　　　　侯門千金待嫁聘，

　　　　　擇婿由天不由人；

　　　　　擇婿由天不由人。

第一場　選匣

(地點：慕容府邸廳堂)

(老管家上，指揮眾人打掃，在紗幕後布置選場)

婢女甲：　(捧金匣過場，唱) 手捧金匣書齋進，

婢女乙：　(捧銀匣過場，接唱) 銀匣添香吐芳馨。

婢女丙：　(捧鉛匣過場，接唱) 鉛匣彩繪托雲錦，

婢女甲、乙、丙：(接同唱) 三個彩匣、彩匣三個呀——主大婚。

(同下)

(鄒梅公子、徐玖參將、芝居浪人、花寶小王爺上)

鄒梅：　　(眉頭深鎖，嘴角下垂，唱) 小生生來一副苦瓜相，

　　　　　　　　　　　　　　　　不憂國民只憂貧。

徐玖：　　(形容猥瑣，歪眼醉步，唱) 任職參將逍遣花酒中，

　　　　　　　　　　　　　　　　千杯不醉日日逢迎。

　　　　　　　　　　　(白) 乾、乾、乾！

芝居：　　(日本浪人，造形誇張，帶日本腔，唱)

　　　　　浪跡天涯任馳騁，

　　　　　武士大刀從來不離身！

花寶：　　(花花太歲，卑鄙下流，唱) 世襲小王是花寶，

　　　　　　　　　　　　　　　　吃、喝、嫖、賭，我全贏。

鄒梅、徐玖、芝居、花寶：(拱手為禮) 請、請。

老管家：　(相迎) 列位請坐。聽說列位都是前來求親的……

鄒梅、徐玖、芝居、花寶：（異口同聲）正是。

花寶：　　（不耐煩地）廢話少說！求親到底有什麼條件，你趕快說來聽聽。

鄒梅、徐玖、芝居：（催促著）是啊，快說、快說。

老管家：　（微微笑著，好整以暇）列位、列位，少安勿躁。慕容老爺遺命，凡來求親者，俱要在金、銀、鉛三個彩匣當中挑選一個。若是選對了，就會看到小姐的畫像。那您可就是姑爺了，可以得到慕容家所有的財產。（語氣轉趨嚴厲）不過，若是選錯了，可就得立即回去，不能透露任何內容，而且要終身不娶。這個約定，列位都聽明白了麼？

花寶：　　（大聲叫嚷）什麼？終身不娶？六妻八妾我還嫌少，竟然要賭小王當和尚？（冷笑）哼、哼，小王不玩了。

　　　　　（拂袖下）

芝居：　　（比手畫腳，帶日本腔）浪人芝居一張大嘴吃四方，可守不住什麼秘密。我也打道回東瀛了。

　　　　　（耍寶下）

　　　　　（鄒梅、徐玖對望一眼）

鄒梅：　　（旁白）三個彩匣？三選一……，這，未免太容易了?!蠢材才選不到哇……

徐玖：　　（旁白）酒力可通神啊。我先喝上八斗再去選，豈有不成之理?!

鄒梅、徐玖：（向老管家）聽得再明白沒有了。快點兒讓我選吧。

老管家：好、好，兩位請隨我來。

　　　　　（老管家引鄒、徐入紗幕後）

〔伴唱〕：一個是醉眼迷矓枉癡想，

一個是挑三揀四甚慌張。

（紗幕後隱約可見二人分別選匣的醜態，二人都沒有選中）

一對兒蛤蟆只把天鵝望，

貪圖家業心不良啊、心不良。

（鄒、徐垂頭喪氣走出紗幕，老管家隨後）

徐玖：　（跟蹌上，接唱）人財兩失悔魯莽，

鄒梅：　（皺眉上，接唱）終究還是白忙一場。

（徐、鄒雙攤手，搖頭嘆氣下。老管家微笑目送）

第二場　借貸

（尼斯府，街道旁）

（索公子、雷公子已在場）

索公子：去年兄弟家有急用，向夏洛借了點銀兩……

雷公子：哎喲！那可使不得。全尼斯府誰不知道這傢伙吃肉不吐骨頭，循環利息可要三分三哩。

索公子：唉，兄弟也是逼不得已。他的手續簡便，取款迅捷啊。

雷公子：索老弟，那你慘了！傾家蕩產也還不清這筆爛賬了！

索公子：原是麻煩得很。未料安兄聽說，竟質押了一艘貨船，派人送來二百兩銀子，解決了兄弟的債務。安兄還不收利息哪。

雷公子：是嘛？安兄對朋友真是沒話說的……

（安員外、巴公子上，分別與索、雷拱手招呼）

雷公子：怎麼啦？安兄，您的臉色不太好，是不是哪兒不舒服啊？

索公子：還是擔憂海外的貨船？……

安員外：（搖搖手，有氣無力的）不、不，雷兄、索兄，不須為我操心。我很好，無有什麼。只是巴賢弟正找我有事，恕我少陪了。

雷公子：安兄不必客氣，咱兩個正好也有事，那就改日再敘吧。

索公子：改日再敘、改日再敘。

（雷、索與安、巴拱手作別下）

安員外：說吧，賢弟，你到底是看中了哪一家的千金？

巴公子：這個麼——

（唱）非是我存心來欺瞞，

　　　　不忍見兄長煩惱添。

（白）大哥，您是明白人——

（唱）小弟我浪費成性散家產，

　　　　負債累累步步艱……

安員外：你還不清楚愚兄的為人嗎？愚兄對你——

（唱）情逾手足知心伴，

　　　　言聽計從另眼看。

　　　　賢弟開懷我春風面，

　　　　賢弟著惱我心頭煩……

（白）到底是怎麼回事兒？你就直說了吧。

（接唱）見不得賢弟愁眉眼，

　　　　　千難萬難、自有愚兄擔。

（白）唉，只要是賢弟開口，一句話，愚兄自當盡力而為。

巴公子：大哥啊——

（唱）鮮花開在貝芒縣，

　　　　豪富能傾半邊天。

　　　　若能訂親門楣換，

　　　　債務清償保平安。

　　　　這門親事雪中炭，

　　　　籌措盤纏左右難。

　　　　還望兄長當機斷，

　　　　助我瑤池把仙品攀。

　　　（白）小弟自信如能（上下比畫）穿戴體面、（擺擺手）
　　　　　　禮數周到，必能得到佳人的青睞。

安員外：你須知愚兄的財產現在都在海上，既無現款也無現貨，一
　　　　　時之間，實在難以籌措銀兩啊。

巴公子：不瞞大哥，小弟也約略知曉。故此昨兒個去了一趟夏公館。

安員外：（驚疑的）什麼？你去找了夏洛？

巴公子：是啊。

安員外：如何？

巴公子：我打算向他借錢。

安員外：唉！糊塗啊！（頓足）你怎麼能向他借錢？他是個放高利
　　　　　貸的大食狗東西啊！

巴公子：小弟何嘗不知?!但是，眼下也只有他有這個能耐呀。

安員外：（搓手）哎呀！

巴公子：他有個條件。

安員外：什麼條件？

巴公子：他要先與大哥參詳。

安員外：哦？——

巴公子：由您擔保。

安員外：（意外的）啊？——

巴公子：故此我才急急地來尋找大哥，問問尊意……

安員外：（非常果決的）就聽賢弟的安排。

巴公子：（愣了一下）大哥您？……

安員外：（更果決的，以手勢示意不必多言）走，你我現在就去找
　　　　　夏洛。

巴公子： （感動的）大哥……

安員外： （拉著巴公子）走吧。

　　　　（安、巴二人圓場，夏洛上）

　　　　（一群孩童圍著夏洛，捉弄他，朝他丟石頭）

孩童： （唱小調）怪老頭、做買賣，

　　　　　　　　走街串巷大搖擺。

　　　　　　　　算盤撥得嘎嘎響，

　　　　　　　　一心要放高利貸。

　　　　（另有一些路人，對夏洛指指點點，面露鄙夷）

　　　　（夏洛驅趕孩童，神色極是惱怒）

夏洛： （唱）老夫放貸六親不認，

　　　　　　不像那假仁假義的中原人。

　　　　　　縱然是一點兒蠅頭小利潤，

　　　　（白）在老夫的眼中呵，

　　　　（接唱）也是相依相親的性命根。

安員外：嘿！（向巴使個眼色，壓低嗓門）那個放高利貸的狗東西
　　　　來了。

巴公子： （提高嗓門，熱情地）夏大老闆，您來得正好。我正要去
　　　　尋您哩。

夏洛： （一面趕人，一面拱手）哦，是巴公子……

　　　　（看到安，旁白）安員外也來了。哼，這個道貌岸然的偽
　　　　君子，瞧他那德行！

巴公子：（拱手為禮）夏老闆，昨天我跟您提過，三千兩銀子……

夏洛：　三千兩銀子，嗯。

巴公子：是呀，借期三個月。

夏洛：　借期三個月，嗯。

巴公子：由安員外擔保。

夏洛：　安員外擔保，嗯。

巴公子：（急切的）您不是說要與安員外參詳麼？

夏洛：　嗯，是要參詳、參詳。（故作沒有看見安員外）

　　　　（旁白）：這個中原人，放貸不收利息，逼得我們大食人
　　　　難做生意啊。最可惡的是，還常常當眾咒罵我的買賣。哼！
　　　　這個偽君子，最好別讓我抓到他的把柄！

巴公子：唔唔唔，安員外就在此處呀（指著安）。夏老闆！

夏洛：　（皮笑肉不笑，向安員外）唷，安員外，您來啦！
　　　　嗯，您和巴公子的交情，大家都是明白的。所以……

安員外：夏老闆，雖然我的借貸一向穩當，從不牟取暴利，也會斟
　　　　酌風險。不過，為了幫忙好兄弟救急，我可以破例。

夏洛：　是啊，破例、破例——老夫也可以破個例……
　　　　（吟）：「凡取與，貴分曉；與宜多，取宜少。將加人，
　　　　先問己；己不欲，即速已……」

安員外：（打斷夏洛，向巴公子）你瞧瞧，賢弟，這個大食人一肚子
　　　　壞水，竟然也會背誦《弟子規》，還高談「汎愛眾」呢。（轉
　　　　向夏洛）喂，我說，你這壞傢伙葫蘆裡賣的是什麼藥啊？

夏洛：　急什麼呀，安員外？三千兩銀子，蠻好的整數。借期三個
　　　　月，這利息麼……

安員外：怎麼？你還想高過三分三嗎？狗東西！

夏洛：　嘿，安員外，您這前前後後咒罵我也不知多少次了。我一
　　　　向都是逆來順受，因為容忍是我們大食人的美德。可今兒
　　　　個嘛，是你們——

　　　（唱）有求於我破天荒，

　　　　　　三千銀兩不平常。

　　　　　　琢磨琢磨細細想，

　　　　　　核計核計也應當。

　　　　　　有話不妨慢慢講，

　　　　　　何必出口就把人傷？

　　　（白）您想想，狗會有錢嗎？狗東西有可能出借三千兩銀
　　　　　　子嗎？

安員外：哼！你這個狗東西！

　　　（唱）放貸謀利沒商量，

　　　　　　人情道義放兩旁。

　　　　　　汲汲營營良心喪，

　　　　　　辱罵於你又何妨！

　　　（白）哼！狗東西！要是你願意借錢，不須當作是借給朋
　　　　　　友。對朋友放高利貸，這算什麼友誼？就當是借給
　　　　　　你的對頭吧。要是他破產了，你也就更易於要求懲
　　　　　　罰。狗東西，吃人的大食人！

夏洛：　唷！瞧您說的！我是想跟您交個朋友，化解以前的冤仇。
　　　　您們不是常說：「己所不欲，勿施於人」嗎？因此，我想
　　　　提供您們的急需，連一毛錢的利息都不要的。您卻不肯聽

　　　　　　我說完。我可是一片好心呢！

巴公子：哦？……這倒是極大的好意。

夏　洛：極大的好意……就「吃人的大食人」而言，對吧？
　　　　　來吧，我們去找個見證，打個合同。
　　　　　嗯，算是開個玩笑吧。（笑）如果您沒有根據合同的期限
　　　　　歸還本金，那麼您要接受的懲罰是──從身上割下一斤肉
　　　　　來。至於要從哪個部位切割嘛，就看老夫高興。（又笑）

安員外：哦？（訝異）──這種合同前所未見，倒是新鮮……（略一
　　　　　思索）好，就此一言為定！算咱看走了眼；你可真是好心。

巴公子：大哥不可、萬萬不可啊。小弟寧可像現在這般窮困潦倒，
　　　　　也不……

安員外：賢弟，且莫擔心。愚兄不會違約的。再過兩個月，愚兄的
　　　　　貨船全部都會進港，（得意微笑）償還借款十幾倍都還綽
　　　　　綽有餘呢。

夏　洛：嘿！瞧瞧這些中原人，自己無情無義，才會懷疑別人的心
　　　　　地！你倒是告訴我：若是他到期還不出錢來，我去要求處
　　　　　罰，又能得到什麼好處？一斤人肉，還比不上一斤牛肉、
　　　　　羊肉值錢呢。不想訂約就算了，請別誤會我的友誼。

安員外：行了，夏老闆，我們去打合同吧。你的好心使你愈來愈像
　　　　　一個知曉禮義的中原人了。

夏　洛：那就走吧。（率先下）

巴公子：小弟還是不放心……

安員外：賢弟不必過慮。愚兄不會有事的。愚兄不是姓安嗎？安啦！
　　　　　（兩人邊說邊下）

第三場　定情

（地點：慕容府邸書齋）

慕容天：（撫琴而歌，唱）

　　　　悶無端、情難已，

　　　　鴛鴦繡罷漫尋思。

　　　　一心願得郎如意，

　　　　恩愛白首不相離。

　　　　怎奈是父命條條須謹記，

　　　　孝悌傳家將我羈。

　　　　怎奈是煙雨霏霏紅滿地，

　　　　春華容易到荼蘼。

　　　　鳳兮鳳兮何所適，

　　　　愁上加愁費猜疑。

　　　　浮生如萍寄，

　　　　但傷知音稀。

〔伴唱〕知音稀。

慕容天：（起身踱步，白）唉！自從爹爹遺命以彩匣招親，不拘是
　　　　什麼王公貴族、三教九流，俱都上門求親。雖非門庭若市，
　　　　也是川流不息。無奈至今尚無一個意中人兒……。好不悶
　　　　煞人也！

〔伴唱〕女兒家心事藏心底，

素情惟有素琴知。

（行雲匆忙上）

行雲：　（口氣急切）小姐、小姐，去年曾隨吳大人一起來拜見老
　　　　爺的那位巴公子——他，他也來求親了。

慕容天：（驚喜狀）巴公子?!（故作鎮定）咦？是哪位巴公子？

行雲：　哎呀，小姐，您也忒健忘了。就是從尼斯府來的那位巴無
　　　　忌巴公子嘛。

慕容天：（故作姿態）哦，是他！

行雲：　是呀，小姐，您想起來了吧？那時，您還稱讚巴公子談吐
　　　　不俗、文采風流呢。

慕容天：這位巴公子，如今在哪裡？

行雲：　他在前廳，由老管家陪著，正要請示小姐，好來選匣子呢。

慕容天：如此，就請他過來吧。

行雲：　是。（欲下）

慕容天：（轉念）且慢！（旁白）萬一、萬一他錯選了彩匣……

　　　　（躊躇、思忖狀）

〔伴唱〕：嬌豔的牡丹雖好戴，

　　　　　要摘也不能摘！

慕容天：（白）啊！有了。

　　　　（提筆賦詩，交予行雲）

　　　　（白）行雲，你將這一花箋送去給巴公子，就說是咱的意
　　　　思，請他暫住府中，仔細端詳，過上幾日再來選匣吧。

行雲：　是。（轉身下）

　　　　（慕容天陷入回憶，隨即嘴角上揚）

〔伴唱〕：伴低粉面斂眉黛，

　　　　　回憶舊時笑顏開。

慕容天：（唱）想當初欲言又止別裙釵，

　　　　　誰料想今日求親上門來。

　　　　　巴郎他品流儒雅令人愛，

　　　　　早已是一抹形影縈心懷。

　　　　　任憑它弱水三千入東海，

　　　　　我只待獨取一瓢共徘徊。

　　　　（行雲復上）

行　雲：　小姐，巴公子還是堅持現在就要來選匣子。他說什麼等待
　　　　　太苦，早選早了。

慕容天：呀！——嗯，既然如此……也罷。

　　　　（暗自沉吟）若他有心，應能找到正確的彩匣……就請他
　　　　過來吧。

行　雲：　是。（下）

慕容天：（祝禱狀，吟）蒼天如有憐人意，莫教楊花任水流。

　　　　（慕容天隱身屏風之後，婢女若干上）

巴公子：（內唱）穿幽徑、繞迴闌——

　　　　（老管家、巴公子、瓜諾、行雲等上）

老管家：巴公子，這廂有請。

巴公子：（接唱）不覺已到畫堂前。

　　　　（一行人魚貫入內）

　　　　　　　紅杏依舊枝頭展，

　　　　彩蝶雙雙舞翩翩。

　　　　前生欠下相思債，

　　　　重訪空谷會幽蘭。

老管家：巴公子，老爺的遺命和選匣的規條，公子想已了然於心；
　　　　　不知公子可能遵守？

巴公子：老管家，但請放心，小生十分清楚這個約定，必會遵守。

老管家：如此，就請挑選吧。

行雲：　（上前）慢著，小姐吩咐，請問巴公子可曾細讀那張花箋？

巴公子：豈只細讀？小生早已銘記在心！

　　　　（吟）真心問取向花箋，

　　　　　　　千里姻緣一線牽；

　　　　　　　有意當然成好事，

　　　　　　　天長地久自纏綿。

　　　　（旁白）看來小姐亦有意於我……只是，這詩的深意麼……

　　　　（尋思狀，喃喃自語）：千里姻緣一線牽……天長地久……

　　　　（漫步到金匣前）：咦？這金匣上頭刻了一句話，我且看
　　　　　　　　　　　　　看是什麼？

　　　　　　　　　　　　「選我者，必獲得眾人所欲。」嗯，
　　　　　　　　　　　　眾、人、所、欲——

　　　　（走到銀匣前）：這銀匣上頭也有一句話呢——

　　　　　　　　　　　　「選我者，必獲得所有應得。」——所、
　　　　　　　　　　　　有、應、得。

　　　　（再快步走到鉛匣前）：這個醜陋的鉛匣，寫得好像不太
　　　　　　　　　　　　　　吉利——

「選我者，必冒險孤注一擲。」

——呀，有意思，頗有意思！

（攤手，唱）：誰不愛金銀珠寶光燦爛，

華彩錦繡日日鮮。

誰不愛佳餚盛饌酒滿盞，

高車駟馬美衣冠。

轉眼間煙消雲散成虛幻，

富貴榮華難上難。

人世真假莫能辨，

天花亂墜總欺瞞。

自古衙門好手段，

矯飾言語是非搬。

懦夫誇勇蘭陵現，

倒戈只在彈指間。

罪惡擅以德行掩，

道貌岸然實藏奸。

外是金玉內敗亂，

細推物理探本原。

我可得——小心謹慎選一選，

成敗全看這一關。

行雲： （揮袖）喂！巴公子，您倒是快快決定呀。

老管家： 公子要選哪一個彩匣啊？

巴公子： （左右端詳三個匣子）這個麼——

（思考、揣度狀）：千里姻緣……一線……牽……

（又看看匣子，似有所悟）：我不要燦爛的金，也不要庸俗的銀。而你（指著鉛匣）你這寒傖的鉛，雖然色澤黯淡，卻勝過花言巧語。我何不冒險孤注一擲？（轉身宣布，果斷地）這就是小生的選擇，祈求天從人願。

（巴公子趨前打開鉛匣，同時慕容天走出屏風）

〔伴唱〕：而今始信春常在，

　　　　　滿園碧綠入窗扉。

慕容天：（喜上眉稍，接旁唱）夫君不是凡俗輩，

　　　　　　　　　　　　　且喜彩匣自為媒。

巴公子：（取出畫像，白）好美的畫像！真是維妙維肖！

　　　　（唱）一雙含情目，

　　　　　　　兩彎柳葉眉。

　　　　　　　面如白花蕊，

　　　　　　　唇似一點梅。

　　　　　　　婀娜多嬌媚，

　　　　　　　風流賽明妃。

　　　　　　　更別有一股子靈秀黠慧，

　　　　　　　顧盼神采飛。

　　　　（白）這畫師真是巧奪天工；丹青素描，點染精妙呵。

　　　　　　　咦？匣內還有一首詩哪。

　　（取詩觀看，吟）形容光彩不足式，

　　　　　　　　　　擇取全憑一片心。

　　　　　　　　　　窈窕佳人歸君子，

　　　　　　　　三生緣定謝天恩。

　　（慕容天款款走近）

行雲、老管家：（躬身行禮）恭喜小姐！恭喜姑爺！

　　　　（瓜諾把行雲拉到一旁，竊竊私語）

巴公子：（行禮）小姐，小生這廂有禮了。

慕容天：（還禮，白）公子！

巴公子：（唱）雲散月明天清朗，

　　　　　　　惺惺相惜如願償。

慕容天：（接唱）今後相敬相體諒，

　　　　　　　事事盤算好商量。

巴公子：（接唱）夫唱婦隨相依傍，

慕容天：（接唱）一切聽憑君主張。

巴公子：（接唱）有難同當福同享，

慕容天：（接唱）再不做嬌生慣養一紅妝。

　　　　（從懷中取出玉戒，白）：郎君呀！今以玉戒作為盟定信
　　　　　　　　　　　物，望君珍藏，切莫小覷。無
　　　　　　　　　　　論如何，萬萬不可變賣、遺失
　　　　　　　　　　　或轉贈，不然，奴家可是不會
　　　　　　　　　　　善罷甘休的。

　　　　（語重心長，唱）翡翠玉戒傳家久，

　　　　　　　　　　　贈予巴郎仔細收。

　　　　　　　　　　　惟願同心永相守，

　　　　　　　　　　　巫山雲雨結綢繆。

　　　　　　　　　　　玉戒若是輕拋售，

海誓山盟付水流，

玉戒只要離你手，

夫妻恩義一筆勾。

巴公子：（接過玉戒）哎呀，小姐，小生當真無言以對了。

（套入手指，唱）：卿卿待我情意厚，

我與卿卿配鸞儔。

（拉起慕容天的手）執子之手偕白首，

生生世世永同修。

（下跪立誓狀，白）皇天后土，實所共鑒：我巴無忌誓不
辜負小姐。但凡還有一口氣在，這個
玉戒，是絕對不會離開小生的。除非，
小生死了……

慕容天：（急掩巴之口，扶起他）啊，郎君，別說這等晦氣之言。
奴家，信得過你。

瓜諾：　（跪下）公子大喜！小姐大喜！小人瓜諾給您們磕頭啦。
衷心祝願兩位白頭到老，早生貴子。只懇求您們在辦喜事
的時候，順帶也讓小的一起娶老婆。

巴公子：哈哈！好啊，只要你找得到老婆。（扶起瓜諾）

瓜諾：　謝謝公子。其實您已經替小的找到了一位。

巴公子：哦？又是哪個？

瓜諾：　小的隨侍公子多年，眼珠子跟您的一樣靈活。您看中了小
姐，我卻瞧見了丫鬟。您談情，我說愛；您沒耽誤時辰，
我也沒浪費光陰。小的使出渾身解數，說得口乾舌燥，總
算得到了這位美嬌娘的同意。正是「一棵樹結兩個果——無

獨有偶」。

慕容天： 行雲，此話當真？

行雲： 是的，小姐，只要您准許。

巴公子： 你呢？瓜諾，婚姻並非兒戲，你可是真心誠意的麼？

瓜諾： （比出誇張的手勢）百分百的真心，公子。

巴公子： 好。那麼，大家同喜吧。我們要大大慶祝一番……

（小廝上，向老管家遞上名帖。老管家略一過目）

老管家： 姑爺、小姐，有一位尼斯府安員外派來的人，他說有緊急要事，要面見姑爺。

巴公子： 哦？（驚疑狀）快快喚他進來。

（慕容天示意行雲一同隱身屏風之後，其他婢女下）

（安泰上，向巴公子行禮）

巴公子： 這不是安泰嗎？

安泰： 是，小人安泰向公子請安。

巴公子： 安泰，你家老爺可好？如此慌張，可有什麼大事？

安泰： 公子有所不知，我家老爺……唉……

（取信交給巴公子）公子請看。

巴公子： （邊折信邊問）怎麼？莫非我那金蘭交生病了麼？

安泰： 唉！老爺無病無痛，但也算不得好。您看信便知。

（巴公子讀信）

慕容天： （旁白）呀，這信看來不妙。巴郎怎麼面容慘白？

（旁白）呀，又彷彿大禍臨頭……

巴公子： 此事當真？

安泰：　一點不假。

巴公子：太離奇了！竟然沒有一艘貨船回來？從蘇丹、方臘、巴里……滿載貨物的船，難道都撞上了礁石不成？他、他、他……他真的血本無歸了麼？

安泰：　可不是麼？一艘都無有哇。而且，就算老爺現有銀兩，那人也不會接受，單單要他的肉！唉，（頓足）這等人我從未見過，長得人模人樣，卻有一副貪婪歹毒的壞心腸。每日家歪纏著包大人，口口聲聲只要討公道。包大人自己和眾多名門仕紳，都去向他說情。但他卻是無動於中，固執得很，聲言合同條款必須條條遵行。

（行雲上）

行雲：　姑爺，小姐有事想和您商量。

巴公子：我也正好有事要同小姐說。

（向安泰）安泰，我已與慕容小姐訂親。你且在府內暫住兩日，待我略作安排，即可啟程。你先下去歇息吧。

安泰：　是。

（老管家招呼安泰下，慕容天上）

慕容天：郎君，究竟發生何事？

巴公子：唉，小姐，此事說來話長啊……

慕容天：不必驚慌，你且慢慢道來。

巴公子：小姐啊——

（嗩吶曲牌，巴公子以身段表示說明前情）

（白）未曾料到……唉，小姐請聽，（讀信）「……愚兄的貨船俱已失事，債主們也愈發兇狠；我跟那大食人的合

　　同已然過期，若要依約行事，愚兄必然喪命。故賢弟所欠，
　　就此一筆勾銷。但求臨終之前能見賢弟一面。惟賢弟若新
　　婚燕爾，有所不便，亦不勉強。……」

慕容天：（旁白）「有所不便，亦不勉強。……」——有何不便呢？
　　　　（白）他欠那大食人多少資費？

巴公子：為了小生，安兄借了三千兩銀子。

慕容天：（忍不住噗哧一笑）什麼？就此區區之數？還他六倍，取
　　　　消那合同。再不，加倍湊個整數，總不能讓朋友有絲毫損
　　　　傷。眼下且遵父命，先把喜事辦了，才能動支庫房。郎君
　　　　放心，一切有我。償清了債務，你可要早些回來。

巴公子：（一揖到地）多謝小姐。小生定會早去早回。
　　　　（切光）

第四場　改扮

（地點：慕容府邸廳堂）

慕容天：……你看，此事……當真沒有問題麼？

行雲：　夫人，不會有問題的啦。姑爺重義氣嘛。

慕容天：只是，夫君匆忙趕往尼斯，神色倉皇，方寸全亂。他對這
　　　　位「安兒」，看來不只是一般的情深義重呢。他……

　　　　（老管家、章成上。老管家先入內）

老管家：夫人，您派到尼斯府去辦事的章成回來了。

慕容天：啊——快叫他進來說話。

　　　　（老管家召章成入內）

章成：　（行禮）小姐——呃，夫人。

慕容天：章成，我讓你去尼斯府採買年貨，你辦得怎樣了？

章成：　回夫人的話，都辦好了。

慕容天：你果然辦事牢靠。辛苦了。等會兒到老管家那裡領賞。

章成：　謝夫人。（欲下）

慕容天：呃，且慢——章成，你在尼斯府，可曾聽到什麼消息？

章成：　夫人不問，小的還不敢說。最近尼斯府出了一樁奇特的公
　　　　案，喧騰得才熱鬧咧。隨便在路上問個不相干的人，都可
　　　　以說上一大篇。

慕容天：哦？什麼公案？

章成：　尼斯府有個大戶安員外，他替朋友借錢作保，用自己的一

斤肉抵押了三千銀兩。如今期限已到，卻還不出錢來，破產了。依照合同上的規定，他的債主——一個名叫夏洛的大食人，要索取他身上的一斤肉作為賠償呢！

慕容天：身上的一斤肉？這豈不是要出人命了嗎？

章　成：是啊。雖然眾人議論紛紛，可也都想不出什麼法子來。再過幾日就要開堂審理，府尹包大人被逼急了，決定派人去都瓦府請託貝可新大人來斷案。包大人相信以貝大人的足智多謀和律法素養，必定可以斷決這個棘手的案件。

慕容天：貝可新？我表兄？他不是正好感染風寒，臥病在床嗎？
　　　　呀！（轉念一想）章成，你一向忠誠老實，我還要讓你去辦件大事，向我表兄要些物件。你且下去歇息片時，咱當修書一封，著你即刻送往都瓦府。不論貝大人交給你什麼文件、衣包，都要立即送到江邊碼頭來。我會先到那裡等你。聽明白了嗎？千萬別誤事。

章　成：夫人請放心，小的自有分寸。（下）

慕容天：來，行雲，沒工夫在此磨蹭了。咱們得上尼斯府找夫君去。

行　雲：他們會見到咱們嗎？

慕容天：會見到的。但咱們要打扮得讓他們認不出來。我需要——
　　　　（唱）換一個、新名姓，
　　　　　　　應對儼然假正經。
　　　　　　　藏起嬌羞主意定，
　　　　　　　且學鬚眉放高聲。
　　　　　　　昂首闊步爭訴訟，
　　　　　　　不動聲色顯才能。

（註：唱此段時，邊學男兒樣；行雲也在旁跟著比畫身段）

行雲：　　那我呢？

慕容天：（接唱）打點齊全圖僥倖，

　　　　　　　　扮成小廝隨我行。

　　　　（白）先這麼著，等會兒在路上，我再把計畫告訴你。現
　　　　　　　在，咱們得趕緊拾掇、拾掇。今天，至少要趕二十
　　　　　　　里的路哪。

　　　　（慕容天、行雲同下）

第五場　折辯

（尼斯府，公堂）

（安員外、巴公子、雷公子、索公子、瓜諾等都已在場，夏洛上）

夏洛：　（得意洋洋，白）這說起來又是椿倒楣的交易，一個破產
　　　　的傢伙——
　　　　哼！（冷笑，唱）揮霍無度一飯桶，

　　　　　　　　　　　　有何臉面上都城？

　　　　　　　　　　　　權當叫化（子）都是命，

　　　　　　　　　　　　叫他當心他的合同。

　　　　　　　　　　　　大搖大擺發號令，

　　　　　　　　　　　　豈知今日要自烹！

　　　　（白）他以前就是喜歡充當大善人；不是借錢給這個，就
　　　　　　　是送糧給那個……總愛批評老夫放高利貸……

　　　　哼！哼！（接唱）叫他當心他的合同，

　　　　　　　　　　　　叫他當心——他、的、合、同。

雷公子：怎麼？如果安員外付不出錢來，你也不致於真要他的肉
　　　　吧？他的肉有什麼用呢？

夏洛：　用來釣魚啊。就算不能用來餵別的，也可以餵餵我的怨懟
　　　　啊。

　　　　（瞥見安員外）哼！這就是借錢不收利息的那個蠢貨。

安員外：請聽我說，好心的夏老闆——

　　　（唱）多年縱橫在商場，

　　　　　　情知賺賠是尋常。

　　　　　　時運不濟甚惆悵，

　　　　　　容我設法作補償。

　　　　　　大發善心功無量，

　　　　　　寬延數日美名揚。

夏　洛：哈！你現在知道我是「好心的」夏老闆啦？你曾經——

　　　（唱）三番兩次無理取鬧，

　　　　　　阻我買賣散錢鈔。

　　　　　　出言譏諷是非挑，

　　　　　　盆盆冷水當頭澆。

　　　　　　千方百計擋財寶，

　　　　　　幸災樂禍把我嘲。

　　　　　　莫怪老夫錙銖較，

　　　　　　禍福皆由你自招。

　　　　　　點點滴滴恨多少，

　　　　　　報應分明在今朝。

　　　（白）哼！你曾經害老夫損失了幾千兩的雪花銀！還到處
　　　　　　挑撥是非，在生意場上孤立老夫。你有什麼理由這
　　　　　　樣做呢？只因為我是個大食人。哼！大食人跟中原
　　　　　　人有什麼不同？大食人就沒有手腳、沒有感覺、沒
　　　　　　有慾望嗎？大食人不跟中原人吃同樣的東西、生同
　　　　　　樣的疾病？大食人——

（唱）大食人平白也會知飢飽，

　　　受欺也會怒火燒。

　　　大食人病痛也要用良藥，

　　　被刺也會魂魄消。

　　　大食人天公地道向誰討？

（白）此仇不報，哼！

（接唱）叫老夫如何發付這滿腹牢騷?!

安員外：夏老闆——

（唱）此一時也彼一時，

　　　大人大量正合宜。

夏洛：　（接唱）老夫已經——（大聲，白）在財神爺面前——

（接唱）發了毒誓，

　　　　絕不放棄興訟詞。

安員外：（接唱）興訟原是不得已，

　　　　　何須仗勢苦苦逼？

夏洛：　（接唱）一切根據白紙黑字，

　　　　　算盤打定不能移。

安員外：（接唱）籌集資金有賢弟，

　　　　　絕不虧欠莫懷疑。

夏洛：　（接唱）簽訂合同豈兒戲？

　　　　　哼！等著打官司、你也莫懷疑！

（白）你以前不是常罵老夫是狗東西嗎？（咬牙切齒）既
　　　然我是狗、東、西，就小心我的尖牙利齒！包大人
　　　一定要給我公道。

安員外：請您聽我說——

夏洛：　我要照著合同來，你不用再囉唆了。我要照著合同來，不必再說了。

（轉身）

巴公子：呸，他這傢伙，簡直是喪心病狂。

安員外：（絕望的）隨他去吧。愚兄絕對不再求懇於他。他分明是故意為難我。往常有人來求我周轉，我是無不應允。為此，眾人方能免於這個大食人的剝削。愚兄心知肚明，他是十分怨恨我的啊。

巴公子：大哥寬心，小弟相信包大人定會為我等做主。

（衙役若干人上。包大人上，坐定）

左右：　威武。

包大人：（驚堂木一拍）傳夏洛。

衙役甲：傳夏洛上堂。

（夏洛上前，參見大人，禮畢）

包大人：夏洛，夏老闆，近前來。

大家都認為，本府也這麼認為，你只是故意擺出這副窮凶惡極的模樣。最後一刻，你應會大發慈悲。換言之，雖然你現在向這個可憐的人索賠一斤肉，不過，你很快就會放棄違約的賠償。而且，基於人性的善良和仁慈，更會免除他的部分本金。他的遭遇，實在令人同情。即便是未受教化的蠻夷，或慓悍頑固的韃靼，再怎麼鐵石心腸的人，都會憐憫他的處境啊。更何況他的朋友已經帶來了銀兩，要還錢予你。

巴公子： 是啊！現在就還給你。

夏洛： 大人，我已經向您表達過我的意願，也在神明面前發過誓，要索取我應得的賠償。若是大人您不答應，那本地的律法，不就成了笑話嗎？

包大人： 夏洛，你為什麼寧可選擇一小塊爛肉，也不願接受三千兩銀子呢？

夏洛： 這個嘛——

　　　　（唱）芝蘭芬芳雖可慕，

　　　　　　　海畔自有逐臭夫。

　　　　　　　有人喜歡臭豆腐，

　　　　　　　有人厭惡烤乳豬。

　　　　　　　有人欣賞俏鸚鵡，

　　　　　　　有人寧願養鷓鴣。

　　　　　　　有人偏好藍配綠，

　　　　　　　有人只要紅帶橘。

　　　　　　　理不清呀千萬縷，

　　　　　　　是非緣由人人殊。

　　　　（白）您若要打破砂鍋問到底，我也沒啥好理由，只能說我對他怨恨難解，厭惡難消——

　　　　（接唱）他是我的眼中釘、肉中刺，

　　　　　　　　他死有餘辜！

巴公子： 你……你真是欺人忒甚！這種回答，你也說得出口！

夏洛： （冷冷的）我的回答沒有必要取悅你。

巴公子：難道看不順眼的，都非得除之而後快嗎？

夏洛：　哈！若不除之，天下還會有「不共戴天之仇」嗎？

安員外：跟這大食人爭辯，還不如與虎謀皮來得容易哪。唉，賢弟
　　　　啊——

　　　　（唱）多言無益枉受辱，

　　　　　　　緣木求魚太糊塗。

　　　　　　　他他他咄咄逼人蠻橫跋扈，

　　　　　　　我我我朝不保夕神思恍惚。

　　　　　　　一肩承擔暗叫苦，

　　　　　　　愚兄好比過河卒。

　　　　（白）唉！不必再浪費唇舌，也不必再想方設法。

　　　　　　　大人，就請依照合同直接判決，讓那大食人稱心如
　　　　　　　意吧。

巴公子：（取出交鈔）欠你三千兩，這裡還六千。

夏洛：　別說六千，就是六萬、十萬，我也不接受。咱們照著合同
　　　　來。

包大人：你這般固執，難道就不怕他人議論麼？

夏洛：　我又不犯法，怕什麼！我向他索取那一斤肉，是花了大錢
　　　　買來的。是我的，我就要。嘿！這尼斯府到底有沒有律法
　　　　呀？我要求判決，哪兒有這麼許多廢話呀！大人，請趕緊
　　　　宣判吧，不要浪費時間了。我還要趕去交易所下單子呢。

　　　　（抽出刀子，用鞋跟磨刀）

包大人：這……

巴公子：你這般磨刀霍霍是何用意？

夏洛：　好從那破產的傢伙身上割肉哇！

巴公子：殘忍的大食人！磨你刀子的不是鞋跟，是你心頭惡毒的恨哪。就連劊子手的斧頭，都不及你的狠毒心腸一半鋒利呢。你對百般求懇都無動於衷麼？

夏洛：　不錯，就憑你的本事肯定辦不到。

　　　　（衙役乙上）

衙役乙：大人，貝大人的專差剛到，他有急件要面呈大人。

包大人：快叫他進來。

　　　　（衙役乙下）

包大人：關於這件案子，本府前些日子已派遣公差去都瓦府，相煩貝可新大人親來審理。

　　　　（專差上）

專差：　參見大人。小的奉貝大人之命，前來呈送文書一封。

包大人：哦，快快呈上來。（看信）原來貝大人身體不適，不克前來，特別推薦了一位幕僚匡先生，代表他來主持審判。來人哪，快快有請匡先生。

衙役甲：是。（出門宣喚）有請匡先生。

慕容天：（內唱）瞞天過海施巧計——

　　　　（慕容天、行雲改扮男裝上）

慕容天：（接唱）不辭辛勞費心機。

　　　　　　　反覆推敲度時勢，

　　　　　　　但願能解燃眉急。

行雲：　（接唱）公堂喬裝易服飾，

　　　　　　　安能辨我是雄雌！

慕容天：參見大人。

包大人：你就是匡先生？

慕容天：正是。這是我的隨從明書。來，見過大人。

（行雲上前施禮，包大人頷首）

包大人：來人哪，看座。

慕容天：謝大人。

包大人：貝大人與本府素有交情；他的學養智謀，本府一向極為推崇。這次貝大人不克親自前來，但在信函中對你讚譽有加，稱許你是少年老成、博學多聞。本府少不得也要倚重了。

慕容天：不敢，但憑大人吩咐。

包大人：先生是否已然了解這案情的整個來龍去脈？

慕容天：學生已然看過宗卷，貝大人也已把他的看法告訴學生。

（面朝外）哪位是安員外？哪位是那大食人——夏老闆？

包大人：安以博、夏洛，近前來。

慕容天：您是夏老闆？

夏洛：　是。

慕容天：您提告的案件確實不尋常，但也合乎律法的規定。以案論案，這也不能怪罪於你。

（向安員外）您的命運操縱於他，是也不是？

安員外：是，他是這般說。

慕容天：您承認有這合同？

安員外：我承認。

慕容天：那麼，這位大食人必須大發慈悲。

夏洛：　為什麼「必須」呢？您有什麼理由？

慕容天： （唱）大慈大悲天下本，
　　　　　　　猶如雨露降凡塵。
　　　　　　　善有善報古明訓，
　　　　　　　典冊記載言諄諄。
　　　　　　　柳毅傳書成合卺，
　　　　　　　漂母一飯值千金。
　　　　　　　一念之間懷惻隱，
　　　　　　　結草銜環報深恩。
　　　　　　　寬容大度留分寸，
　　　　　　　得饒人處且饒人。
　　　　　　　即便訴求要公允，
　　　　　　　法理人情宜酌斟。
　　　　　　　顧全仁義盡本分，
　　　　　　　勸君三思存哀矜。

　　　　　（白）說了這許多，無非想勸你不要堅持討公道。你若執
　　　　　　　意如此，根據律法，本人必須做出不利於安員外的
　　　　　　　判決。

夏洛：　我的賬算在我頭上！我要的是律法，我那合同上訂的違約
　　　　條款。

慕容天：他難道無力償還那筆借款？

巴公子：有啊，我在這裡當場交付予他——雙倍的銀兩。如若那還
　　　　不足，我情願以自己作為抵押，償還十倍。如若這還不夠，
　　　　顯然就是惡意占了上風。那我懇求您，就這一回，用您的
　　　　職權強制律法，為小惡以救大善，莫讓這殘忍的禽獸一意

孤行。

慕容天：這不可行。尼斯府無權改變既定的律法。任意破例，日後只會造成更多的紛爭。絕對不可。

夏洛：　好個青天！真是個好樣兒的！啊，不愧是青年才俊，老夫佩服！

慕容天：請您讓我看看那紙合同。

夏洛：　在這裡，先生，就在這裡。

慕容天：夏老闆，有三倍，甚至更多的銀兩，要還你呢。

夏洛：　發過誓的，我在財神爺面前發過誓的。把整個尼斯府給我也不幹。

慕容天：唉，這合同過期了。根據律法，這個大食人有權要求一斤肉，任他在欠債者的胸膛上割下來。發發慈悲吧，收下三倍的錢，讓我撕了這合同。

夏洛：　那得先據條件還了債才行。看來您的確精通律法，令人欽佩。我依照律法向您請求，您就逕行判決吧。我堅持依約行事。

安員外：我也誠心請求您下斷。

慕容天：如此──（眼眸一轉，下定決心）您必須敞開胸膛挨他的刀。

夏洛：　啊，公正的先生，了不起啊。

慕容天：因為律法的意涵和精神，完全符合這一紙合同所記載的違約處罰。

夏洛：　對極了。您真是正直又有智慧！不像外表這般稚嫩。

慕容天：故此您要祖露胸膛。

夏洛：　對，他的胸部。合同這麼寫的，對吧？尊貴的先生。「緊、貼、其、心」：一字不差。

慕容天：果然。這裡可有個秤來秤肉的重量？

夏洛：　已經備下了。

慕容天：夏老闆，您去喚個大夫來替他療傷，以免他因失血過多一命而亡。

夏洛：　合同上可有約定？（伸手取回合同，閱讀）

慕容天：未曾明言。但有何妨？就算做件善事。

夏洛：　老夫找不到，沒有寫在合同上。

慕容天：至於您，安員外，您有何交代？

安員外：唉。寥寥數言罷了，我已然作好準備。

　　　　賢弟呵——

　　　　（唱）我運數已定劫難逃，

　　　　　　　命懸一線如紙鷂。

　　　　　　　巴山夜雨空憑弔，

　　　　　　　置酒相待隨風飄。

　　　　　　　四顧茫然仰天笑，

　　　　　　　甘願為弟把心掏。

　　　　　　　從此徘徊黃泉道，

　　　　　　　也免得落拓潦倒、晚景淒涼、苦受煎熬。

　　　　　　　勸賢弟你不必自責懊惱，

　　　　　　　對弟妹也莫要隱瞞分毫。

　　　　　　　義結金蘭對天表，

　　　　　　　兄弟一場生死交。

巴公子：（唱）大哥為我難周全，

　　　　　　　小弟揮淚愧無言。

　　　　　　　雖然新婚多繾綣，

　　　　　　　難忘結拜在當年。

　　　　　　　膠漆相投情匪淺，

　　　　　　　悲憤無已問蒼天。

　　　　（白）唉！

　　　　（接唱）悔不該娶親貝芒縣，

　　　　　　　驀然平地起波瀾。

　　　　　　　何惜嬌妻共家產？

　　　　　　　恨只恨不能代兄赴黃泉！

　　　　（安、巴二人抱頭痛哭）

慕容天：（旁唱）原指望月老已將紅繩繫，

　　　　　　　正慶幸終身有託情不移。

　　　　　　　如今是難捨難分賢棠棣，

　　　　　　　似拋卻信誓旦旦的結髮妻。

　　　　　　　霎時間五味雜陳偷眼覷，

　　　　　　　顧不得冷言冷語反脣譏。

　　　　（白）尊夫人如果在場，可是不會感謝你的唰。

瓜諾：　小的也已娶妻，小的也很疼老婆。但我現在寧願她掛了，

　　　　到西天去求佛祖庇佑，改變這個狼心狗肺的大食人。

行雲：　（旁白）還好你是背著她說的，要不然——就要仔細你的

　　　　皮了。

夏洛：　我們在浪費觀眾的時間，請您判決吧。

慕容天：本人裁決，那安員外的一斤肉是你的；律法有明文規定。

夏洛：　最最公正的先生！

慕容天：您可以從他的胸口割下這塊肉；律法是這麼容許。

夏洛：　最最博學的先生！宣判了。來，（在兩手吐上唾沫）呸！
　　　　呸！咱得準備好。

　　　　（切光）

（中場休息）

第六場　判決

（尼斯府，公堂）

夏洛：　我們已經浪費觀眾不少時間了，請您判決吧。

慕容天：本人裁決，那安員外的一斤肉是你的；律法有明文規定。

夏洛：　最最公正的先生！

慕容天：您可以從他的胸口割下這塊肉；律法是這麼容許。

（示意衙役架起安員外，扯開外襟）

夏洛：　最最博學的先生！宣判了。來，（在兩手吐上唾沫）呸！
　　　　呸！咱早就準備好啦。

　　　　（舉起刀）來吧！

　　　　（正要刺進安的胸膛時，猶豫了一下。眾人倒抽一口氣。
　　　　肅靜。巴公子掩面不忍看，慕容天冷眼旁觀。夏洛再舉起
　　　　刀，正要刺下）

慕容天：且慢！還有話講。

　　　　這紙合同可沒有說要給你一滴中原人的血啊。白紙黑字，
　　　　寫得明明白白，是「一、斤、肉」。照合同來吧。你就拿
　　　　走你那斤肉，不過——割肉的時節，假若你灑了被告的一
　　　　滴血，你的土地和家產，根據律法，都要全部充公。

　　　　（全場突然鴉雀無聲，接著一片譁然，爆出叫好聲）

瓜諾：　啊，正直的先生！
　　　　聽好了，大食人——啊，博學的先生！

夏洛：　這是律法嗎？

慕容天：你自己來看這條律例。

　　　　（夏洛趨前看）

　　　　你既然堅持要依法行事，包管你吃不完兜著走。

瓜諾：　啊，博學的先生！

　　　　聽好了，大食人——正直的先生！

夏洛：　那我接受這個價碼。付三倍的銀兩，就放了這個中原人。

巴公子：錢在這裡。

慕容天：且慢。

　　　　要給這個大食人完完全全的公道。且莫心急。

　　　　什麼也不給他，只能照合同來。

瓜諾：　哎呀，大食人。好個公正的先生！博學的先生！

慕容天：現在，你去割下那塊肉吧。不能流血——

　　　　（唱）不能流血當堂論，

　　　　　　　分寸拿捏要小心。

　　　　　　　多少丁點兒不含混，

　　　　　　　恰恰只有整一斤。

　　　　　　　天平兩端不對稱，

　　　　　　　哪怕誤差一毫分，

　　　　　　　沒收財產言有信，

　　　　　　　可別怨我太偏心。

瓜諾：　青天再世！是個青天，大食人！你這個傢伙，我可逮著你
　　　　啦。

慕容天：大食人，怎麼不動啦？去拿你該拿的呀。

夏洛：　　（棄刀於地）還我本金，讓我走。

巴公子：早已備下了；拿去。

慕容天：他早已當堂拒絕這個安排。就給他公道和合同上所寫的一斤肉。

瓜諾：　青天哪，我還是要說，青天再世！

夏洛：　　難道我連本金都拿不回來麼？

慕容天：你什麼都不能拿，除了合同上寫的。拿的風險由你自己承擔，大食人。

夏洛：　　（撿刀凝視，再凝視安、慕容、包大人；緩緩轉身凝視場上眾人；嘆氣頓足，隨即棄刀）那，那就便宜他吧。我不告了。

慕容天：不忙，不忙，大食人，還有另一筆賬要跟您算。尼斯府的律法明確記載：如若有哪個外地人意圖謀害本地人的性命，不論是自己動手或教唆殺人，他所圖謀的對象就可以取得他一半的財產，另外一半則收歸府庫。而這個主謀的性命，全憑府尹大人發落，不得再有異議。本人宣布這就是你目前的處境。從本案審理的程序看來，你分明是蓄意謀害被告，在場的都是人證。故此，跪下吧，去向府尹大人求情。

瓜諾：　求大人准許你上吊吧——不過，你的財產已經要充公，你連買根繩子的錢都沒有……唉，只好花納稅老百姓的錢把你吊死。

包大人：為了讓你明白我們中原文化講究忠恕之道，你毋須求情，本府直接饒了你的性命。至於你的財產，一半給安員外，

　　　　　另外一半繳納府庫。若是你恭敬服從，或可減為罰鍰。

夏洛：　免了，拿走我的身家性命吧，不必留了。您奪走我的財產，
　　　　就是判我死刑啊。

慕容天：安員外，（揮手示意衙役鬆綁）您會給他何等的慈悲呢？

安員外：哦，我同意公家那一半減為罰鍰，但可不是我的那一半。
　　　　而且，他要立刻歸化中土，不再穿著奇裝異服。

包大人：他必須照辦，不然，本府就收回先前的特赦。

慕容天：滿意麼？大食人，你還有何言語？

夏洛：　唉！（旁唱）離絕域、到中原、越過千山和萬水，

　　　　　　　白手起家、謹小慎微。

　　　　　　　晝夜不休心勞瘁，

　　　　　　　外地經商能靠誰？

　　　　　　　年年繳納苛捐雜稅，

　　　　　　　人前人後把小心陪。

　　　　　　　身為異族非同類，

　　　　　　　遭受排擠淚暗垂。

　　　　　　　忍氣吞聲等機會，

　　　　　　　好容易——今朝終於辨是非。

　　　　　　　我只道十拿九穩萬事備，

　　　　　　　磨刀霍霍爐火炊。

　　　　　　　誰知曉風雲變色成譎詭，

　　　　　　　煮熟的鴨子啊、撲喇撲喇喇喇展翅飛。

　　　　　　　三倍的銀兩好實惠，

　　　　　　　親手推卻悔難追。

　　　　　高利放貸功虧一簣，

　　　　　樂極竟然也生悲。

　　　　　精打細算全枉費，

　　　　　完美的合同與願違。

　　　　　事到如今知難退，

　　　　　老夫唯有賠本歸。

　　（白）我⋯⋯接受，我⋯⋯無話可說。

　　　　　　包大人，我忽覺身體不適。望求大人准我先行告退。

包大人：你下去吧。

　　　　　（夏洛行禮後，蹣跚下）

包大人：（驚堂木一拍）退堂。

　　　　　（眾人正步出公堂，慢動作幾秒鐘。燈光打在慕容天身上；
　　　　　慕容面無喜色，心事重重）

包大人：匡先生，請留步。

　　　　　本案多虧先生，方能圓滿。本府將於後堂設宴，為先生洗
　　　　　塵；請留下一敘，本府還要多多請教。

慕容天：多謝大人。然則貝大人另有公務交辦，學生必須立即趕回
　　　　　都瓦府。尚祈大人鑒諒。

包大人：既有公幹，本府亦不便強留。那，就請代為問候貝大人。
　　　　　改日本府再去拜望。

慕容天：是，學生一定轉陳。

包大人：（轉向安）安員外，你可要好好答謝匡先生啊。

安員外：是、是，送大人。

　　　　　（包大人下，眾人步出公堂）

第七場　致謝

（尼斯府，公堂外）

巴公子：可敬的先生，由於您的機智，我等才能免於性命之憂。
　　　　（取出交鈔）這是原來要還給那大食人的三千銀兩，謹此
　　　　轉贈先生，聊表謝意。望先生萬勿推卻。

安員外：是啊，先生的大恩大德，我是沒齒難忘。日後如有需要，
　　　　請隨時吩咐。赴湯蹈火，在所不辭。

慕容天：不才淡泊名利，從來不圖錢財。這次能有機會為兩位消災
　　　　解厄，也是註定的緣分。順利解決了此案就好。些須小事，
　　　　不勞掛心。（稍頓，意有所指）但願下回相見，還能相認。
　　　　兩位保重，就此告辭。

巴公子：呃，先生，恕我冒昧。無論如何，請收下一些禮品。且莫
　　　　當作報酬，權當是個紀念。

慕容天：（略一遲疑）您既如此誠心，也好。
　　　　（指巴公子的手指）這個戒指，可否送給我作個紀念？

巴公子：這個戒指麼？（遲疑，縮手）哎呀，這不值什麼，太寒傖
　　　　了……不成敬意啊。

慕容天：是麼？我倒覺得它的色澤晶瑩圓潤，頗有君子之風。就這
　　　　個戒指吧。

巴公子：這個戒指並非價格特別高昂，只是對我而言意義重大，難
　　　　以割捨。如蒙先生不棄，當另選一名貴寶戒奉贈。（低頭

視戒）至於這一個麼，恕我委實難以從命。

慕容天：哦，我明白了。您說來甚是大方容易，敢麼是先教我怎麼當個叫化子，再教我如何打發叫化子。

巴公子：不不不，先生誤會了。這個戒指是拙荊的饋贈。我曾發誓絕不離手的。

慕容天：這個藉口甚好，可以省卻送禮的麻煩。尊夫人如能識得大體，就會明白這戒指我是多麼受之無愧。告辭。

　　　　（慕容天故示鄙夷，然後轉向行雲，頷首暗笑。兩人下）

安員外：好兄弟，且把這個戒指送給他吧。他可是愚兄的救命恩人哪。

巴公子：這個麼……

安員外：（唱）　自從賢弟前程登，

　　　　　　　　愚兄強顏心不寧。

　　　　　　　　貨船失事無蹤影，

　　　　　　　　合同到期暗自驚。

　　　　　　　　各處借貸多不應，

　　　　　　　　坐困愁城白髮生。

　　　　　　　　求告債主遭譏諷，

　　　　　　　　無端惹來一身腥。

　　　　　　　　噩夢連連總不醒，

　　　　　　　　夜夜糾纏到天明。

　　　　　　　　滿腹辛酸如泉湧，

　　　　　　　　慨嘆無窮誰與聽？

　　　　　　　　萬念俱灰捨性命，

　　　　卻不想——絕路又逢生。

　　　　玉戒固然為誓證，

　　　　畢竟只是一玲瓏。

　　　　救命恩情如山重，

　　（白）賢弟啊，他救的可是**我的命**哪！

　　（接唱）難道還抵不過、區區一情盟?!

巴公子：（唱）安兄所言亦成理，

　　　　本當奉贈不猶疑。

　　（舉起手，正欲脫下戒指，又停住）

　　（旁唱）惟恐娘子不體己，

　　　　嗔怨於我她不依。

　　（沉吟半晌，旁白）這便如何是好？

　　（伴唱）一個是情深義重好兄弟，

　　　　一個是才貌雙全美嬌妻。

　　　　取捨之間多顧忌，

　　　　何去呀何從、患得又患失……

安員外：（催促著）賢弟，趕快把戒指送給匡先生吧！不然，他可就走遠了。

巴公子：這個……

　　（看看戒指，看看安員外；又看看戒指，再看看安員外，神情非常苦惱）

安員外：賢弟啊……

巴公子：（終於下定決心）也罷。

　　（接唱）事事豈能盡如意？

回報大恩不宜遲。

（脱下戒指，白）瓜諾，快快趕上前去，把這個戒指交給匡先生。

（切光）

第八場　協議

（貝芒縣，慕容府邸廳堂）

慕容天：（唱）耳邊廂只聽得風雨浪浪，

　　　　　　　是這般夜深沉好不淒涼。

　　　　　　　一陣陣錐心痛無以名狀，

　　　　　　　怪只怪夫君他做事荒唐。

　　　　　　　對天地發誓願恩情全忘，

　　　　　　　更不顧定情時我語重心長。

　　　　　　　到如今多情怎對薄情講，

　　　　　　　一腔哀怨、一腔哀怨意徬徨。

（凝視著手中的戒指）

　　　　　（白）實實令人難以相信……原以為……卻又竟然……如

　　　　　　　此輕易……

（行雲托茶盤上）

行雲：　是啊，夫人。沒想到瓜諾這個奴才，竟也學起姑爺來。不

　　　　過說了幾句閒話，就把我給他的定情戒指，也轉送給那個

　　　　我假扮的隨從了。（頓足）好惱啊！

慕容天：行雲，待等他們回來，咱們非問個清楚不可！

（老管家上）

老管家：啟稟夫人，姑爺和他的朋友回來了。

慕容天：說我出迎。

老管家：（向外宣告）夫人出迎。

　　　　　（慕容天、行雲等出迎，同時巴公子、安員外、瓜諾等上。
　　　　　雙方行相見禮，入內）

慕容天：夫君，歡迎回府。

巴公子：多謝娘子。

　　　　呃，娘子，容我引見一位摯友。來，就是這位，這位就是
　　　　安兄——我的大哥，他的深情厚意，我永遠也無法回報。

慕容天：（翩然施禮）安兄長！歡迎光臨寒舍。安兄的恩德，小妹
　　　　早已聽聞，確實是難以回報。

　　　　（行雲拉起瓜諾的手，到一旁低聲交談）

安員外：（還禮）弟妹忒客氣了！

巴公子：幸好如今一切都已圓滿解決。

瓜諾：　（向行雲，大聲）我對天發誓，你冤枉我了！天地良心啊！
　　　　我真的是把它給了匡先生的隨從。看你，生那麼大的氣！

慕容天：怎麼啦，行雲？吵什麼呀？這麼沒規矩，讓客人笑話！

巴公子：不妨，大哥不是外人。

安員外：是啊、是啊，愚兄不是外人，弟妹不要見外才好。

慕容天：既這麼著，那麼，瓜諾，你先說。

瓜諾：　夫人，為了一個金戒指，她給我的，一個值不了多少錢的
　　　　小玩意兒。上面刻了兩句辭兒，天下隨便哪個工匠都會刻
　　　　的。

行雲：　你還記得刻的是什麼辭兒嗎？

瓜諾：　不就是什麼「相知相惜，不離不棄」嗎？

行雲：　哈！虧你還記得！

　　　　（唱）說什麼「相知相惜不離不棄」，

　　　　　　　八字箴言值幾文？

　　　　　　　當初是你發議論，

　　　　　　　戒在人在獻殷勤。

　　　　　　　轉眼毀約又背信，

　　　　　　　還敢夸言嚼舌根？

　　　　　　　移情別戀不承認，

　　　　　　　編造藉口搪塞人。

　　　　　　　誰是誰非你捫心問，

　　　　　　　有理無理啊，老天為我指迷津！

瓜諾：　我發誓，我給的是個小廝，匡先生的隨從。個子矮矮的
　　　　——咦，就跟你一般高。他唧唧喳喳的，啥都不要，就只
　　　　要這個戒指作為報酬。不給他，說不過去，才給了他。

慕容天：瓜諾，這就是你的不是了。定情信物，難道是可以隨便送
　　　　人的麼？何況，你還發了誓，要永遠珍藏。莫怪行雲這般
　　　　生氣。要是換了我，還不知是多麼惱怒呢。

巴公子：（旁白）哎呀，糟了。我最好把這截指頭剁了，再發誓是
　　　　為了保衛那失去的戒指。

瓜諾：　可是，我家公子也把他的戒指送給了匡先生，匡先生也的
　　　　確當得起。後來，他的隨從，就是跟前跟後的那個，也來
　　　　向我討。他們兩個啥都不要，偏只要這兩個戒指。我也沒
　　　　法子呀。

慕容天：哦？夫君，你給了哪個戒指？該不會是我送的那一個吧？

巴公子：呃，娘子，實不相瞞，正是那一個。我也是情非得已啊。

慕容天：情非得已？哼！（拂袖）

巴公子：娘子息怒，且聽我說。

　　　　唉！若你知道我是送給了哪一個，為了哪一個而送，為了什麼原因送，又是在多麼不捨的情況下送，就不會這般惱怒了。

慕容天：哼，若你想想這個戒指有多麼珍貴，是哪一個送給你的，你應該多麼珍惜，就不會這麼輕易送人了。

巴公子：娘子啊——

　　　　（唱）那日在公堂之上險象生，

　　　　　　　我也曾不甘示弱據理爭。

　　　　　　　無奈何法有明文寬濟猛，

　　　　　　　無奈何大食狗賊鐵心橫。

　　　　　　　一紙合同一條命，

　　　　　　　全仗匡君立大功。

　　　　　　　三千紋銀權酬贈，

　　　　　　　他卻只對、這個玉戒情獨鍾。

　　　　　　　我也曾百般猶疑、舉棋不定，

　　　　　　　思前想後、顧慮又重重。

　　　　　　　為的是安兄待我情義盛，

　　　　　　　忘恩負義啊、天地也不容。

　　　　（白）娘子，當真是事出有因呵。

慕容天：（唱）定情玉戒非罕見，

　　　　　　　夫君盟誓若等閒。

　　　　　生死相隨到永遠，

　　　　　句句是你親口言。

　　　　　而今輕捨此物件，

　　　　　是否別有女嬋娟？

　　　　　莫不是朝三暮四初心變？

　　　　　莫不是鸞鳳求凰化雲煙？

　　　　　莫不是真情如夢難檢點？

　　　　　莫不是花不常開月難圓？

　　　　　果然是夫妻之間情緣散，

　　　　　我又何必在乎──那一圈！

瓜諾：　　（噗哧一笑）哈，那一圈！那──一──圈！哈哈哈！

巴公子：（瞪他一眼）虧你還笑得出來！

慕容天：（眼眸一轉）

　　　　　（白）一般君子怎會要你這個物事？那人必然是個女子唷。

巴公子：不是呀，娘子，千真萬確，那不是個女子呀。如若你當時
　　　　在場，一定也會讓我把玉戒送給匡先生的。

慕容天：那敢情好！夫君既然送了玉戒，怎不連我一起送哇？

行雲：　　對呀，也把我送給他的隨從好了。我會很高興跟他同床共
　　　　枕！

瓜諾：　　（忿忿然）哼，別給我逮著了，否則──我就把他閹了。

安員外：唉，這些爭吵都是因我而起……

慕容天：安兄長，請勿介意，您可是寒舍的貴賓呢。

巴公子：好娘子，且饒了這一遭，我發誓以後不敢了。（打躬作揖）
　　　　卑人在此賠禮了。

慕容天：列位都聽見了？他又發誓了……

巴公子：呃，娘子，（下跪立誓狀）皇天后土，實所共鑒：我巴無
　　　　忌誓不辜負娘子。日後如有負心，教我天打雷劈。

安員外：呃，弟妹，愚兄曾以一斤肉質押，為他借錢，幾乎喪失性
　　　　命；而今，愚兄情願再以十斤肉作保，保證巴賢弟今後絕
　　　　對不會故意違背誓言哪。

慕容天：如此兄長必須充當他的保人。（取出玉戒）把這個給他。
　　　　叫他比以前那個更小心收藏。

安員外：巴賢弟，（轉交玉戒）這回你可要仔細了。

巴公子：是是是！但凡我巴無忌還有一口氣在，這個玉戒，是絕對
　　　　不會從我的手上脫下來的……（細看玉戒）

　　　　（行雲也取出金戒交給瓜諾）

行　雲：你也要小心保管。

巴公子：看哪，這就是我給匡先生的那一個！

慕容天：可不！這是匡先生給我的定情物呢。

行　雲：親愛的瓜諾，這也是那矮冬瓜隨從給我的唷。

瓜　諾：嘿！這可是烏龜配著忘八家，咱們都戴綠帽子啦。

慕容天：不許胡說。

　　　　（得意）我想，你們都弄糊塗了吧。唔，這裡有一封信，
　　　　是我表兄——都瓦府的貝大人寫的。你們看了就會明白。
　　　　其實，我就是匡先生，行雲就是他的隨從啊。

　　　　（舞台上眾人皆驚）

安員外：竟有這等事！

巴公子：（打量她）你是匡先生？我竟沒認出來？

瓜諾： 你就是那個要我戴綠帽的隨從？

行雲： 是啊。

巴公子：哈哈哈……娘子啊，（一揖）匡先生，上次的喜事辦得匆忙，不夠隆重，咱們再重來一次可好？

（慕容天斜睨他一眼，似笑非笑，不置可否）

（巴公子上前欲摟慕容天，慕容天略作閃避身段；瓜諾摟著行雲，雙雙下。獨留安員外在場黯然神傷）

安員外： （唱）往事已矣不堪回首，

姻緣分明木成舟。

丹心一點向誰剖？

百般無奈萬事休。

金石情誼化烏有，

恨不能一場大醉解千愁。

（切光）

尾　聲

（婚禮，安員外等眾人在場觀禮。巴公子與慕容天、瓜諾與行雲上，雙雙行禮。拜完天地，夫妻交拜時，慕容天未拜，定格）

〔伴唱〕：譜新詞、叶雅韻，

　　　　　一曲《約／束》自沉吟。

　　　　　人間情義有時盡，

　　　　　天涯何處覓知音？

　　　　　縱然律法斷公允，

　　　　　何須追究苦認真？

　　　　　癡情空留千古恨，

　　　　　一輪明月照天心。

劇　終

精選曲譜
Selected Scores

樂譜繕打　丁一雷

情難已
Unnamable Ennui

古箏 獨奏

作曲 耿玉卿

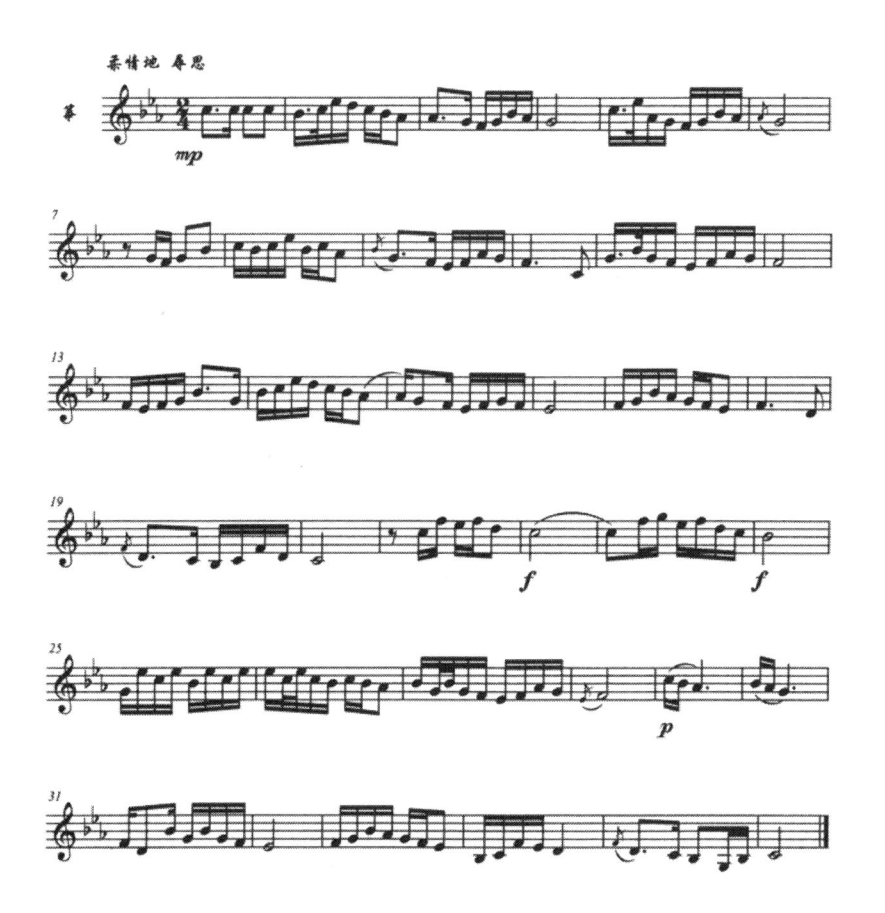

悶無端 情難已
Unnamable Ennui

慕容天 獨唱

作曲 耿玉卿

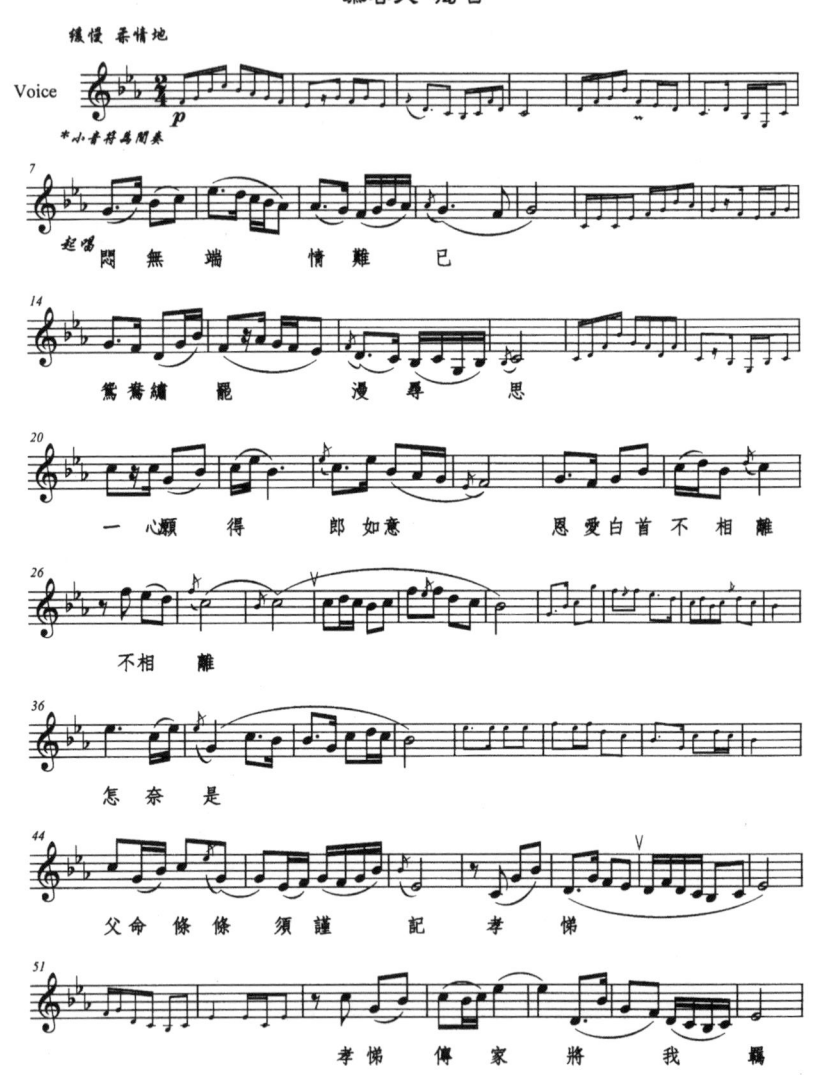

怎奈是 煙雨霏霏紅滿地　　春華 容易 到茶

蘼

鳳兮鳳 兮 何所 適愁上加

愁 寶猜 疑　　浮生如萍寄 但 傷知音

稀　　（伴唱）但傷知音 稀

女兒家心 事

藏心底　　素情惟有素琴知 惟 有

素琴 知

rit.

成敗全在這一關
Failure or Success

巴無忌 獨唱

作曲 耿玉卿

一雙含情目
Eyes Beaming with Love

巴無忌 獨唱

作曲 耿玉卿

是非緣由人人殊
Reasons Differ

夏洛 獨唱

作曲 耿玉卿

大慈大悲天下本
The Base of Humanity

慕容天 獨唱

作曲 耿玉卿

不能流血當堂論
Shed No Blood

慕容天 獨唱

作曲　耿玉卿

Voice

*小音符為間奏　f

起唱

不能 流 血 當 堂 論

分寸拿捏 要小 心 多 少 丁 點兒

不含 混 恰恰只 有

可是整 一 斤 天平兩端不對稱 哪怕誤差

一毫分 沒收財產言有信 可別怨 我

嘿嘿 太偏 心 哪

樂極竟然也生悲

Pleasure Turns to Grief

夏洛 獨唱

作曲 耿玉卿

忍氣吞聲 等 機會 好容易

好容易 今朝終於 辨是非 辨是非

我只道 十拿九穩萬事備 磨刀霍霍

磨刀霍霍爐火炊 爐火炊

誰知曉 風雲變色 成譎詭

煮熟的鴨子呀

撲喇喇展翅飛 展 翅 飛呀

三倍的銀兩 好實惠呀 親手推卻 悔難追

救命恩情如山重
A Large Favor

安員外 獨唱

作曲 耿玉卿

到 天 明 滿 腹 辛 酸 如 泉 湧 箇 中 折

磨 誠 無 窮

萬 念 俱 灰 捨 性 命 卻

不 想 卻 不 想 絕 路 又 逢 生

又 逢 生

玉 戒 固 然 為 誓 証 畢 竟 只 是 一 玲 瓏 賢

弟 呀

他 救 可 是 我 的 命 我 的 命 啊

難 道 還 抵 不 過

區 區 一 情 盟

左至右（left to right）：
王海玲飾夏洛/Hai-Ling Wang as Xia Luo (Shylock)
蕭揚玲飾慕容天/Yang-Ling Hsiao as Murong Tian (Portia)
朱海珊飾安員外/Hai-Shan Chu as Master An (Antonio)
劉建華飾巴公子/Chian-Hua Liu as Master Ba (Bassanio)

王海玲飾夏洛，朱海珊飾安員外，蕭揚玲飾慕容天

直影馨西神準韻

直影新闽美演樑式之一

直影新闽美演樑式之二

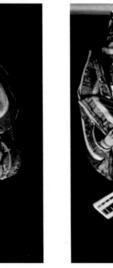

安員外與巴公子的深情表現

夏洛全盤皆輸

織布的賽德克婦女

劇終謝幕者

BOND

A Bangzi Opera adapted from
William Shakespeare's
The Merchant of Venice

by
Ching-Hsi Perng and Fang Chen
English Translation by Ching-Hsi Perng

STUDENT BOOK CO., LTD.

BOND

A Bangzi Opera adapted from
William Shakespeare's *The Merchant of Venice*
by Ching-Hsi Perng and Fang Chen
English Translation by Ching-Hsi Perng

Copyright©**Student Book Co., Ltd.** 2009
All rights reserved.
No.11, Lane 75, Sec. 1, He-Ping E. Rd., Taipei, Taiwan
http://www.studentbook.com.tw
email: student.book@msa.hinet.net

ISBN 978-957-15-1479-6

Translator's Note:

It is with great pleasure and most sincere gratitude
that I record here my indebtedness to
Professor Tom Sellari, of National Chengchi University,
Taiwan, and
Mr. Joseph Graves, Artistic Director of Peking University's
Institute of Theater and Film.
They read earlier versions of the English translation
with loving care and critical acumen, and offered a wealth of
useful suggestions for improvement,
most of which have been incorporated here.
Any infelicities that remain are of course solely my
responsibility.

Two scenes—"The Debate" and "The Sentence"—from the play were performed by Taiwan BangZi Company on 11 September 2009 at Greenwood Theatre, King's College London, as part of the program of "Local/Global Shakespeares," The Fourth British Shakespeare Association Conference, 11-13 September 2009.

Director	*Po-Shen LU*
Associate Director	*Ching-Chun YIN*
Xia Luo	*Hai-Ling WANG*
Master Kuang / Murong Tian	*Yang-Ling HSIAO*
Ba Wuji	*Chian-Hua LIU*
An Yibo	*Hai-Shan CHU*
Mingshu / Xingyun	*Wen-Chi HSIEH*
Gua Nuo	*Chang-Min HU*
Judge Bao	*Ching-Chun YIN*
Guard	*Yu-Ting WU*
A Saracen	*Chi-Ching YANG*

The play in its entirety premiered on 28 November 2009 at City Stage, Taipei, Taiwan.

The play was performed on 7 April at Bellevue, Washington, U.S.A., as part of the program of The Thirty-Ninth annual conference, Shakespeare Association of America.

And then it was performed on 12 April at Mendelssohn Hall of The University of Michigan, Ann Arbor, and on 15 April at Scranton Cultural Center, Scranton, U.S.A.

Director	*Po-Shen LU*
Associate Director	*Ching-Chun YIN*
Xia Luo	*Hai-Ling WANG*
Murong Tian (Master Kuang)	*Yang-Ling HSIAO*
Ba Wuji	*Chian-Hua LIU*
An Yibo	*Hai-Shan CHU*
Xingyun (Mingshu)	*Wen-Chi HSIEH*
Gua Nuo	*Hsiao-Wei CHENG*
Judge Bao	*Ching-Chun YIN*
Master Lei	*Yung-Wei LIN*
Master Suo	*Chin-Chung CHANG*

Old Steward	*Hui-Chen LIEN*
An Tai	*Ya-Chen HSIAO*
Zhang Cheng	*A-Chun WU*
Composer	*Yu-Ching GENG*
Musical Arrangement	*Ting-Ying ZHANG*
Costume Design	*Heng-Cheng LIN*
Light Design	*JACK*
Stage Design	*Hui CHEN*

List of Characters

Xia Luo   A Saracen who has amassed his wealth through
                 usury

Murong Tian   A rich lady in Beimang County

Ba Wuji   A poor gentleman from the Prefecture of Nisi

An Yibo   A business tycoon in the Prefecture of Nisi

Xingyun   Murong Tian's lady-in-waiting

Gua Nuo   Ba Wuji's servant

Judge Bao   Prefect of Nisi

Master Kuang   Assistant to Prefect Bei Kexin of Duwa (Murong
                 Tian in disguise)

Mingshu   Master Kuang's servant (Xingyun in disguise)

Master Lei   Master An's friend

Master Suo   Master An's friend

Old Steward   Steward of the Murong household

An Tai   Master An's servant

Zhang Cheng   A servant in the Murong household

Messenger   In the service of Master Bei

A number of suitors for Murong's hand

A number of maidservants in the Murong household

A number of children in Nisi

A number of men in the street

Attendants and guards of the court

List of Scenes

Prologue

(Location: the reception room of the Murong mansion, in Beimang County)

(Enter several maidservants, busy with chores.)

(Chorus, *offstage*):

> **Absurdities abound throughout this world;**
> **By a dead father's will her life is bound.**
> **Alas, the magnate's daughter cannot choose**
> **Her mate; alas her mate she cannot choose.**

Scene 1: The Caskets

(*Location: the reception room in the Murong mansion*)

(*Enter* Steward, *who supervises some servants in cleaning up and setting up the selection scene behind a screen.*)

1ST MAID: (*carrying the gold casket, sings*)

I bring the casket gold into the studio.

2ND MAID: (*carrying the silver casket, sings*)

The silver casket gives off fragrance.

3RD MAID: (*carrying the lead casket, sings*)

On finest motley silk the casket lead is laid.

ALL THREE: (*sing in unison*)

Three colored caskets, oh, three caskets shall decide our lady's mate.

(*Exeunt.*)

(Enter suitors: Scholar Zou Mei, the Frowner; Lieutenant general Xu Jiu, the Imbiber; Shibai, *the Japanese Wanderer; and Grandee* Hua Bao, *the Spender.*)

ZOU: (*his brows knitted, grimacing, sings*)

Born with a screwed-up face,

All I care about is my wealth.

XU: (*Wretchedly soused, sings*)

>A soldier by profession, I delight in women and wine;
>
>I've the capacity of an ocean, so let's drink, drink,
>
>drink!

SHIBAI: (*pretentiously dressed, sings with a Japanese accent*)

>I wander the four seas as a loner,
>
>My bed-fellow being this samurai sword.

HUA: (*knavishly, sings*)

>A hereditary prince, I pride myself
>
>On wining and dining, gambling and womanizing.

ZOU, XU, SHIBAI, HUA: (*politely to each other*) After you, after you.

STEWARD: (*greeting them*) Please be seated, honorable guests. I understand you are here to court our lady . . . .

ALL FOUR: (*in unison*) Yes, indeed.

HUA: (*impatiently*) Let's get to the point. How can we win the lady? Tell us your conditions!

ZOU, XU, SHIBAI: (*hurrying*) Yeah, speak, speak!

STEWARD: (*smiling, and taking his time*) Honorable guests, my honorable guests, no need to rush. According to the will of my deceased Master Murong, anyone who comes courting must choose between the gold, silver, and lead caskets. He that makes the right choice will find our lady's portrait in the casket. He then will be his son-in-law, and can inherit all the fortunes my late master left behind. *But (turning serious)*—if

you make the wrong choice, you have to depart immediately, keep secret your choice, and never woo a lady to marry her. These are the terms.—Are they clear?

HUA: (*Hollering*) What? Never marry? Six wives and eight concubines I consider nothing, and you want me to risk being a bachelor my entire life? (*grinning sardonically*) Humph! I'm not playing.

(*He leaves in anger.*)

SHIBAI: (*gesturing with his hands, speaks in Japanese accent*) I depend on my big mouth wherever I go. I cannot keep any secret. I'm going back to Japan.

(*Exit clownishly.*)

(Zou Mei and Xu Jiu *look at each other.*)

ZOU: (*aside*) Three caskets? One out of three . . . Hmm, that's a piece of cake! Only a fool could miss it. . . .

XU: (*aside*) Liquor be my inspiration! Eighty liters of wine will lead me to success!

ZOU AND XU: (*to* Steward) It is perfectly understood. Now let us choose. Quick!

STWARD: Sure, sure. This way please.

(Steward *leads them to the room behind the screen.*)

(Chorus, *offstage*):

This one is a bleary-eyed lunatic,

That one, a panicky, fussy fruit.

(Through the screen is vaguely shown the two suitors' antics in choosing the casket. Neither succeeds.)

(Chorus, *offstage*):

A pair of toads is yearning for the swan:

Their evil goal is Murong's fortune—nothing else.

(Zou *and* Xu, *in utter frustration, walk out from behind the screen, followed by* Steward.)

XU: *(enters staggering, picks up the aria)*

Neither lady nor money have I gained,

ZOU: *(enters frowning, picks up the aria)*

When all is said and done, it's a waste of time!

(Exeunt Xu *and* Zou, *sighing in despair, as* Steward *watches, smiling.)*

Scene 2: The Loan

(Location: a street in Nisi Prefecture)

(Master Suo *and* Master Lei *are talking to each other.*)

SUO: Last year I had urgent need of money, so I borrowed from Xia Luo . . .

LEI: Oh no! Didn't you know that this guy takes the bone with the meat when he eats? He charges compound interest at 33 percent!

SUO: Alas, I had no other choice. He had cash in hand and there was no red tape.

LEI: Then you're done for! Now you'll never be able to get rid of this debt!

SUO: It would have been terrible. But who would have guessed that, when Master An heard about this, he pawned a ship of his and sent me two hundred taels of silver, interest-free, to clear my debt to Xia Luo!

LEI: Is that so? Nobody beats Master An when it comes to friendship . . . .

(*Enter* Master An *and* Master Ba. *They greet* Lei *and* Suo.)

LEI: How now, Master An? You don't look well. Are you alright?

SUO: Or perhaps your mind is tossing on the ocean . . .?

AN: (*waving his hand, feebly*) No, no, Masters, don't worry about me. I'm fine. It's nothing, really. But Master Ba here wants to discuss something with me. Would you excuse us?

LEI: Sure, Master An. We happen to have some business at hand too. Let's catch up some other day.

SUO: Some other day, some other day.

(Lei *and* Suo *bid* An *and* Ba *goodbye. Exeunt.*)

AN: Now tell me, my dear brother, which lady has so enchanted you?

BA: Well—

(*sings*)

> **Never did I intend to keep this from you, but**
>
> **I couldn't bear to burden you with worries more.**

(*speaks*) Big brother, you know perfectly—

(*sings*)

> **A spendthrift, I've squandered all my property.**
>
> **So deep in debt that I can hardly . . .**

AN: You know me well. To me you are—

(*sings*)

> **A bosom friend, much dearer than a sibling.**
>
> **I listen to you and can deny you nothing.**
>
> **When you're happy, I rejoice for you;**
>
> **When you're worried, my heart sinks.**

(*speaks*) So, what is it? Speak!

(*resumes singing*)

> **I just can't bear to see you sad.**
>
> **Whatever burden, I'll shoulder it for you.**

(*speaks*) Ah, just tell me what it is, and I'll do my best to help you.

BA: My dear brother—

(*sings*)

> **In Beimang County blooms a beauty rare,**
>
> **Whose wealth, all told, would rival half the world's.**
>
> **To win her hand could change my fortunes now,**
>
> **Could clear my debts and keep me safe and sound.**
>
> **This marriage offers timely help I need.**
>
> **No money have I for the journey there.**
>
> **Oh, would you, please, oh, please, be generous**
>
> **And help me win her in that fairyland.**

(*speaks*) I'm confident that, had I but the means to furnish myself with decent dress and lavish gifts, I could win the lady!

AN: You know all my fortunes are at sea; I don't have any money at present, or even a way to raise some.

BA: Indeed, dear brother, that's what I thought. So I paid a visit to Master Xia.

AN: (*taken aback*) What? You went to see Xia Luo?

BA: Yes.

AN: And—

BA: I've decided to borrow money from him.

AN: Are you out of your mind? (*stomps a foot*) How could you borrow from him—from that loan dog, that Saracen Shark?

BA: I know, but at this moment he alone can come up with the money.

AN: (*wringing his hands*) Aiya!

BA: There's a condition though.

AN: What condition?

BA: He wants to talk to you first.

AN: Eh?—

BA: You must be guarantor of the loan.

AN: (*surprised*) Oh?—

BA: That's why I'm in such a hurry to seek you out—to ask for your . . .

AN: (*very resolutely*) As you wish.

BA: (*stunned for a second*) My dear brother?

AN: (*even more resolute*) It's alright. Come on, let's go find Xia Luo.

BA: (*touched*) Dear brother . . .

AN: (*dragging* Ba) Let's go.

(An *and* Ba *pace around stage. Enter* Xia Luo.)

(*A group of children surround* Xia Luo, *teasing him and throwing*

stones at him.)

CHILDREN: (*singing a ditty*)

> A lunatic, strutting as he goes,
>
> A heartless dealer everybody knows.
>
> Click-clack, click-clack now sounds his abacus;
>
> That shark from Saracen, that damned old cuss.

(*Some passers-by point fingers at him, showing contempt.* Xia *angrily shoos the children.*)

XIA: (*sings*)

> When making loans, I have no relatives.
>
> Why be a hypocrite, the Chinese way?
>
> A profit, even one of a fly's-head size,

(*speaks*) in my eyes,

(*sings*)

> Is critical to my dear livelihood.

AN: Hey! (*winks at* Ba *and whispers*) Here comes that dog, that loan shark.

BA: (*raises his voice, warmly*) Well met, my dear Master Xia! I was just on my way to see you.

XIA: (*greets* Ba *while shooing away the children*) Well, so it's you, Master Ba . . . (*catches sight of* An, *aside*) Master An is here too. Humph! This sanctimonious hypocrite, how disgusting he looks!

BA: (*greets* Xia *formally*) Sir, as I mentioned to you yesterday, the

three thousand taels of silver . . .

XIA: Three thousand taels of silver. Well.

BA: Yes, sir, for three months.

XIA: For three months. Well.

BA: And Master An will sign the loan.

XIA: Master An will sign. Well.

BA: (*eagerly*) Didn't you say you would talk to Master An about it?

XIA: Hmm, we shall talk. (*pretends not to see* An)
(*aside*) This Chinese local, he lends out money gratis, making it difficult for us Saracens to do business here in Nisi. Worst of all, he often berates me and my business in public. Humph! I'd like to fix his Cathayan clock!

BA: (*points to* An) Well, well, well, Master An is right here. Do you hear, Master Xia!

XIA: (*feigning a smile, to* An) Ah, well, Master An, so you're here! Hmm, who doesn't know how close you are to Master Ba? So . . .

AN: Master Xia, I've always been conservative. I never charge or give excessively when lending or borrowing, and I always take the risk into consideration. Yet, to supply the urgent need of my good friend, I'll break a custom.

XIA: Ah yes, break a custom, break a custom—I might also break a custom . . .

(*recites*)

"In giving and taking, there's much wisdom:

"Be generous when giving; be moderate when taking.

"Before imposing on others, remind yourself first:

"If you don't like it done to you, cease doing it to others."

AN: (*interrupting* Xia, *to* Ba) Mark you this, my brother, this evil Saracen Shark can recite our *Instructions to the Youth*. He can talk nobly about "love for all"! (*turning to* Xia) Hey you, what do you mean to do by all this?

XIA: Take it easy, Master An. Three thousand taels of silver; it's a good round sum. For three months. The rate, well . . .

AN: What? Do you mean to raise it higher than 33 percent? You currency cur!

XIA: Listen, Master An, many a time and oft you have berated me. Still have I borne it with a patient shrug, for long suffering is the badge of Saracens. Well then—

(*sings*)

> **It now appears you need my help: a first!**
>
> **Three thousand taels of silver, no small sum.**
>
> **This has to be considered carefully,**
>
> **The numbers all meticulously summed.**
>
> **Softly and slowly when you speak; do not**
>
> **Insult me every time you ope your mouth.**

(*speaks*) Stop and think when you call me a dog, a shark.

Does a dog have money? Can a silver shark lend three thousand taels of silver coin?

AN: Humph! You dog!

(*sings*)

> **Most unrelenting, money lending dog,**
>
> **You know no kindness or true equity;**
>
> **You trade your soul, your conscience, for mere gain:**
>
> **It is most fit to call you demon names!**

(*speaks*) Humph! Your cur! If you'll lend the money, lend it not as a friend, for what friend ever took such outrageous interest for a loan? Lend it rather as to your enemy. For if an enemy defaults, you can with good conscience exact the penalty—dog, shark, Saracen!

XIA: Listen how you rage! I want to be friends with you, and reconcile our differences. Doesn't your old saying go, "Do not do to others what you do not want done to you"? I agree with that. That's why I'd like to lend you the money, interest free, no charge; but you won't listen till I finish. I mean well.

BA: What? . . . uh, that is a most kind offer.

XIA: Most kind . . . for a Saracen Shark, eh?

Come with me to the notary, we'll sign the papers.

And . . . just for fun (*laughing*), if you do not repay me not on the day we specify, we'll cut a pound of your flesh from what part of your body pleases me. (*laughs again*)

AN: Huh? (*surprised*)—I never heard of anything like that. It's crazy! . . . . (*pauses a moment in thought*) All right, it's a deal! I was mistaken. There's much kindness in you.

BA: No! My dear brother, you shall not sign such a bond for me. I'd rather not get the money than . . .

AN: Don't worry, dear brother; I won't forfeit. Within two months, all my cargo ships will return. (*smiling complacently*) and then I can easily repay ten times this loan.

XIA: Hey! Look at these Chinese, whose own hard dealings teach them to suspect the thoughts of others! Please, tell me this: If he should forfeit the loan, what on earth would I gain by getting a pound of human flesh? It would not be worth so much as a pound of beef or mutton. If you don't want to take my offer, then forget it. I'm just trying to be friendly, that's all.

AN: All right, Master Xia, let's go sign the papers. You're more and more like the civilized Chinese: you grow kind.

XIA: Let's go then. (*exit*)

BA: I don't like this deal . . . .

AN: Don't worry. I know what I'm doing. Don't I always come through for you . . . for everyone?

(*Exeunt, talking.*)

Scene 3: Bonding of Love

(*Location: a study in the Murong mansion*)

MURONG: (*zither in arms, sings*)

> Unnamable ennui and unceasing yearning.
> Done with embroidery of paring ducks,
> Oh, how I long for him, the perfect mate.
> To love and cherish and never to part.
> But duty binds me, my family code;
> I must obey all my dead father's will.
> Withered flowers carpet earth in misty rain:
> Alas how spring's beauty soon comes to ruin!
> Oh, Phoenix, Oh, Phoenix, Oh where will you go?
> Uncertainty heaps grief on grief on grief.
> Like duckweed on water our lives surely drift.
> How sad that true love's hard to find!

(Chorus, *offstage*):

> True love's hard to find!

MURONG: (*gets up and paces around, speaks*)

Alas! Since this choosing a husband by caskets according to
Father's will began, all kinds of people have come to court.
It's almost as crowded as the marketplace with all the men

streaming in. And yet so far I've not found a suitor to my liking. . . . How frustrating!

(Chorus, *offstage*):

> **A girl's own thoughts are harbored in her breast;**
> **Alone the zither knows her feelings, pure.**

(*Enter* Xingyun *in a hurry*.)

XINGYUN: (*in an eager tone*) Madam, madam—Master Ba, who came last year with Lord Wu to visit your father—he, too, has come!

MURONG: (*pleasantly surprised*) Master Ba?! (*composing herself*) Uh? Which Master Ba?

XINGYUN: Oh dear! You are so forgetful! The man who came last year, Master Ba Wuji, from the prefecture of Nisi.

MURONG: (*as if recalling*) Oh, now I remember.

XINGYUN: Yeeess, madam, now you remember, eh? You used to praise him for his elegant conversation, literary talent, and graceful appearance.

MURONG: This Master Ba, where is he now?

XINGYUN: In the anteroom, attended to by the old steward. He is about to ask for your permission to choose the casket.

MURONG: Well, then, bring him here.

XINGYUN: Yes, ma'am. (*about to leave*)

MURONG: (*changes her mind*) Wait! (*aside*) And yet, what if . . .

what if he should choose the wrong casket? . . . (*hesitating and pondering*)

(Chorus, *offstage*):

> **A gorgeous peony makes a great headdress,**
>
> **But isn't for just anyone to pluck!**

MURONG: (*speaks*) Ah, I've got it. (*picks up the brush and composes a letter in the form of a verse, which she hands to* Xingyun) Take this letter to Master Ba. Say it is my wish. Ask him to tarry a few days and take a look around before choosing the casket.

XINGYUN: Yes, ma'am. (*exit*)

(Murong *deep in memory; a half-smile crosses her face.*)

(Chorus, *offstage*):

> **Her head bent, her brows knit,**
>
> **She smiles as memories of old return.**

MURONG: (*sings*)

> **About to mutter something when he left,**
>
> **Now come again to court me face to face.**
>
> **The graceful Master Ba I so adore;**
>
> **He long has left his impress fair on me.**
>
> **Of all the water flowing in the sea**
>
> **I drink but single cup, if it be he.**

(Xingyun *re-enters.*)

XINGYUN: Your ladyship, Master Ba insists on choosing the casket right now. He says waiting is too much suffering, and he would like to get it over with as soon as possible.

MURONG: Oh?—Well, if he insists, . . . so be it.

(*muttering to herself*) If he is earnest, he should be able to pick the right casket. . . . Bring him in.

XINGYUN: Yes, ma'am. (*exit*)

MURONG: (*praying, recites*)

Heaven, be merciful, do not

Abandon willow flowers to the river.

BA: (*off-stage, sings*)

Through quiet path, round winding railings here—

(*Enter* Steward, Master Ba, Gua Nuo, Xingyun, *etc.*)

STEWARD: Master Ba, this way please.

BA: (*continues singing*)

We're suddenly arrived at painted hall,

(*as they enter the hall one by one*)

Where rosy apricots show off in trees

And butterflies dance gracefully in pairs.

In former life I caught love's rare disease,

It leads through quiet dale to orchid rare.

STEWARD: Master Ba, I'm sure you know of my late Master's will and the rules about choosing the caskets. Can you abide by

them?

BA: Yes, please rest assured that I am very clear about the contract and will abide by its articles.

STEWARD: If so, please make your choice.

XINGYUN: (*coming forward*) Tarry a little. My lady asks if Master Ba has carefully perused her letter.

BA: Peruse it? I've carved it in my heart!

(*recites*)

> **A truthful heart, who reads this letter, will**
>
> **Be linked with her heart, as if by a thread.**
>
> **While destiny makes suitor lady's thrill,**
>
> **Their love will last while on this earth they tread.**

(*aside*) It appears the lady is well-disposed to me . . . but, as to the exact meaning of the poem . . .

(*in deep thought, muttering to himself*) "Be linked with her heart, as if by a thread, . . . while on this earth they tread . . ."

(*ambles to the gold casket*) Eh? There's a sentence carved on the gold casket. Let me see what it says. "Who chooseth me shall gain what many men desire." Hmm. "*what—many—men—desire.*"

(*walks to the silver casket*) There's also a sentence on the silver casket: "Who chooseth me shall get as much as he deserves"—"*as—much—as—he—deserves.*"

(*marches to the lead casket*) The sentence on this unseemly

lead casket doesn't seem to bode well: "Who chooseth me must give and hazard all he hath." Hey, this is interesting, quite interesting!

(*sings*)

> **Who loves not shining gold and brilliant gems,**
> **Or splendid brocade fabric for his use?**
> **Who loves not dainty dishes, cups of wine,**
> **Or handsome chariots and gorgeous clothes?**
> **In twinkling, oh, they melt into thin air;**
> **Illusive are high ranks and wealth and fame.**
> **So may the outward shows be least themselves:**
> **The world is still deceived with ornament.**
> **The court has long been known as such a place**
> **Where perjury and falsehood do prevail.**
> **Oft cowards brag of bravery unmatched,**
> **Yet they surrender 'fore the battle's joined.**
> **Oft vice assumes some mark of outward good,**
> **And treachery is masked by sober brows.**
> **Look into ornament and grossness see:**
> **This law discover and then search for truth.**
> **In choosing, I too careful cannot be;**
> **On this depends my failure or success!**

XINGYUN: (*waves her hand*) Well, Master Ba, please make your decision now.

STEWARD: Which casket do you choose?

BA: (*surveying the three caskets*) Well—

(*pondering, appraising*): "Be linked with her heart, as if by a

thread, . . . by . . . a . . . thread . . ."

(*looks at the caskets again; as if enlightened*): I will have

neither the gaudy gold nor the common silver. But you,

meager lead, though gloomy in hue, surpass flattering

eloquence. Why don't I give and hazard all? (*turns around

and announces, resolutely*) Here choose I; joy be the

consequence!

(Ba *goes forward to open the lead casket as* Murong *comes from

behind the screen.*)

(Chorus, *offstage*):

> **Not until now did I believe that spring would last:**
>
> **A gardenful of green encroaches at the pane.**

MURONG: (*overjoyed, picks up the aria, aside*)

My husband is no common sort;

The casket's made a happy match!

BA: (*takes out the portrait*) What a beautiful portrait! It looks just

like her!

(*sings*)

> **A pair of eyes that beam with love,**
>
> **Her curving brows like willow leaves;**
>
> **Her face a bud's own pistil white,**

Her lips a single plum flower;

So graceful and so charming, she

Surpasses legend's great beauties.

A kind of unique wisdom too

Does spirit up her looks.

(*speaks*) A marvelous piece of painting: What demi-god has come so near creation! What? A poem in the casket?

(*recites the poem*)

"All that glitters is not gold;

"With your heart you did behold.

"The lady fair you may enfold

"Then thank God for this love foretold."

(Murong *approaches gracefully.*)

XINGYUN and STEWARD: (*bowing down*) Hearty congratulations to your ladyship! Hearty congratulations to your lordship!

(Gua Nuo *pulls* Xingyun *to one side; they whisper to each other.*)

BA: (*bows*) Madam, here are my respects.

MURONG: (*returns the salute*) My lord!

BA: (*sings*)

The clouds thus all dispersed, show a clear moon.

The dream of kindred spirits is fulfilled.

MURONG: (*sings to the same tune*)

Henceforth with shared respect and sympathy

Shall we two carefully lay plans as one.

BA: (*sings to the same tune*)

'Twixt husband and his wife, reigns harmony.

MURONG: (*sings to the same tune*)

In everything my lord shall have last word.

BA: (*sings to the same tune*)

We'll share and share alike—hardship and ease.

MURONG: (*sings to the same tune*)

No more a pampered girl will this girl be.

(*produces a jade ring from her bosom, speaks*) Now, my dear lord, this jade ring shall be the witness of our bond of love. It is no small matter, mind you; please take heed that you guard it well. Never shall you sell, lose, or give it away, or I will never forgive you.

(*sings, in earnest*)

This emerald ring, an heirloom of our house,

I give as keepsake to my noble lord.

Forever may our loving hearts be bound

And love between our hearts continue to grow.

But if or when someday this jade ring's lost

So lost become our vows of solemn love,

The parting of this ring from this your hand

Our bond as man and wife does countermand.

BA: (*taking the jade ring*) Ah, madam, I am made speechless.

(*slips the ring on his finger, sings*)

> **As my dear wife I know your love is true,**
>
> **So I forever will be true to you.**

(*holds* Murong's *hand*)

> **Your hand in mine, we'll grow together old;**
>
> **And never part through lives lived manifold.**

(*kneels down to make a vow*) Heaven and earth be my witness:
I, Ba Wuji, hereby swear never to disappoint my lady. As
long as I can breathe, this ring shall never part from me.
Unless I die . . .

MURONG: (*muffles Ba's mouth in a hurry and helps him up*) Oh my
dear lord, never utter such terrible words. I have faith in you.

GUA NUO: (*kneels down*) Hearty congratulations to my lord! Hearty
congratulations, my gentle lady! I kowtow to you, sincerely
wishing you two everlasting love, and that you will soon
beget children. When your honors decide to solemnize the
bargain of your faith, I do beseech you, even at that time I
may be married too.

BA: Ha, ha! Very well—as long as you can find a wife. (*helps Gua
up*)

GUA: I thank your lordship, you have found me one.

BA: Oh? Who is she?

GUA: Having served you all these years, my eyes, my lord, can look
as swift as yours. You saw the mistress, I beheld the maid.
You loved, I loved. I can't wait any longer than you, my Lord.

For wooing here until I sweat, and swearing until my mouth was dry, at last I got a promise of this fair one here. As the saying goes, "One tree bears two fruits—good things come in pairs."

MURONG: Is this true, Xingyun?

XINGYUN: It is, madam, if it pleases you.

BA: And do you, Gua Nuo, mean good faith? Marriage is no trifling matter.

GUA: (*gestures exaggeratedly*) 100 percent, my lord!

BA: Well, then, let's celebrate together. We will have two most merry marryings. . . .

(*Enter a servant, submitting a calling card to the* Steward, *who glances at it.*)

STEWARD: My lord and my lady, there's a messenger from Master An of the Prefecture of Nisi. He says he has an urgent message for my lord.

BA: Oh? (*astounded*) Bring him in, quick!

(Murong *signals* Xingyun; *they hide behind the screen. Exeunt the other maids.*)

(An Tai *enters and bows to* Ba.)

BA: Isn't this An Tai?

AN TAI: Yes. Your servant An Tai greets your lordship.

BA: An Tai, how is your Lord?—You look nervous. What's the matter?

AN TAI: My lord, well, you . . . Lord An my master . . . (*sighs; gives* Ba *a letter*) Please read this.

BA: (*asks as he opens the letter*) How now? Can it be that my best friend is ill?

AN TAI: Alas! He is not sick, my lord, but he is not well either. You will understand when you read the letter.

(Ba *peruses the letter.*)

MURONG: (*aside*) Oh, there must be some terrible news in that paper. See how it steals the color from my lord's cheek.

BA: Can this be true?

AN TAI: Nothing truer.

BA: This is unthinkable! All of them? From Sudan, Sumatra, Bali . . . how could all his ships run into rocks? Is he . . . is he . . . is he really totally ruined?

AN TAI: He is! Not even one ship returned. Besides, even if he had the money now, that Saracen would not take it. He wants flesh! (*stomps his foot*) I've never seen such a creature: one that assumes a human shape but is all malice inside! He implores Judge Bao morning and night for what he calls "justice." Judge Bao himself, and the other dignitaries, have tried to persuade him to be reasonable. But no one can dissuade the Shark from demanding the bloody restitution. He is adamant

that the exact demands of the bond be followed.

(*Enter* Xingyun.)

XINGYUN: My lord, my lady would like to have a word with you.

BA: And I have something to tell her too.

(*to* An Tai) An Tai, I'm engaged to Lady Murong, the lady of the house here. Stay here for a couple of days while we make arrangements and then we will leave together. Now go and take some rest.

AN TAI: Yes, sir.

(Steward *leads* An Tai, *exeunt. Enter* Murong.)

MURONG: My lord, what exactly is it?

BA: (*sighs*) Madam, it's a long story. . . .

MURONG: Take it easy. Tell me everything.

BA: Ah, my lady—

(*Suona (horn) music. Ba tells the story by gestures and movements; then speaks*)

Never would I have thought . . . Alas, listen to this: [*Reads*] "My ships have all run aground, my creditors grow cruel, my estate is very low, my bond to that Saracen is forfeited; and since in paying it, it is impossible I should live, all debts are cleared between you and me, if I might but see you at my death. However, if this should prove inconvenient to you, being newly wedded, do not force yourself to come."

MURONG: (*aside*) "if this should prove inconvenient to you . . . do not force yourself . . . ."—what does this mean?

(*speaks*) How much does he owe that Saracen?

BA: For me, brother An borrowed three thousand taels of silver.

MURONG: (*breaks into laughter in spite of herself*) What? No more? Pay him six times, and tear up the bond. Or double that, before your friend shall lose a hair. First let's follow Father's command and get married, so that we may use the money. Set your mind at ease, my dear lord; just leave things here to me. But make sure that you return as soon as the debts are cleared.

BA: (*bows low*) Thank you, precious Lady, very much. I shall be back soon.

(*Light dims.*)

Scene 4: The Disguise

(Location: the reception room in the Murong mansion)

MURONG: . . . About this, . . . do you really think there's nothing
fishy?

XINGYUN: No, madam, absolutely nothing. My lord is just, a man of
loyalty.

MURONG: And yet, he left for Nisi in such a rush, hurry-scurry.
Absolutely panicky. It looks like there's more to his loyalty to
this "big brother" than meets the eye. He . . .
(Enter Steward *and* Zhang Cheng. Steward *hurries into the
room.)*

STEWARD: Madam, Zhang Cheng, whom you sent to Nisi on
business, has returned.

MURONG: Ah—call him in this minute.

(Steward *summons* Zhang.)

ZHANG: *(bows)* What's your wish, Madam?

MURONG: Zhang Cheng, what about the supplies for the new year
that I asked you to purchase in Nisi?

ZHANG: All set, Madam.

MURONG: You are dependable, as always. Thank you. You may
collect the reward for your pains from the steward.

ZHANG: I humbly thank you. (*starts to leave*)

MURONG: Ah, wait a minute—Zhang Cheng, what's the news in Nisi?

ZHANG: Yes indeed. Recently there's been a strange lawsuit there, stirring quite a lot of noise and excitement. Ask anyone in the street there and he will overwhelm you with his version of the story.

MURONG: Oh? What kind of suit?

ZHANG: There's one Lord An, a very wealthy man in Nisi. He pawned a pound of his own flesh for a loan of three thousand taels of silver for his friend. The time is up and he cannot come up with the money. He's broke. And according to the bond, his creditor, a Saracen by the name of Xia Luo is now seeking a pound of Lord An's flesh!

MURONG: A pound of flesh from his body? Wouldn't that kill him?

ZHANG: I dare say. But even though there's been much talk about this, nobody can come up with a solution. The case will be heard in a few days. Judge Bao, hard pressed, has sent for Lord Bei Kexin, Prefect of Duwa, for help, confident that the resourceful and learned Lord Bei can solve this difficult case.

MURONG: Lord Bei? My cousin? I thought he was under the weather and bedridden. Well! (*an idea occurs to her*) Zhang Cheng, as you've always been honest and faithful, I have another important mission for you. I want you to get some

articles from my cousin. Go take some rest while I write a letter, which you shall deliver to my cousin in Duwa. Whatever he entrusts to you, make sure you take to the wharf, where you shall meet me. Is that clear? Don't delay.

ZHANG: Please rest assured, madam. I know my duty. (*exit*)

MURONG: Come, Xingyun, there's no time to be lost. We shall see our husbands in Nisi.

XINGYUN: Shall they see us?

MURONG: They shall. But we will dress in such as way they shall not recognize us. I must—

(*sings*)

> **Go by a brand new name, that's what I'll do,**
>
> **And put on sober airs and somber looks,**
>
> **Conceal my shyness and stand fully firm.**
>
> **Then my voice raise as any gent might do,**
>
> **With stride so masculine, stride into court,**
>
> **Win case with manly wit, and female guile.**

(*acting like a man as she sings, with* Xingyun *shadowing her*)

XINGYUN: What about me then?

MURONG: (*continues with the aria*)

> **Get everything all ready, pray for luck,**
>
> **Disguise yourself as my page, follow me.**

(*speaks*) Enough for now. I'll tell you the whole plan on the way. Let's hurry and get ready, for we must travel twenty

miles today.

(*Exeunt.*)

Scene 5: The Debate

(*Location: law court of the Prefecture of Nisi*)

(Master An, Master Ba, Master Lei, Master Suo, Gua Nuo *and others are already in the court. Enter* Xia.)

XIA: (*glowing complacently, speaks*) This is in fact another bad match: a bankrupt—humph!

(*sneers, then sings*)

> **A prodigal, a good-for-nothing,**
> **Dares show his head here in the capitol!**
> **A stroke of luck has rendered him a beggar.**
> **Let him look to his bond.**
> **Where are the smug commands of yesterday?**
> **How could he know that death demands today?**

(*speaks*) He was wont to play the philanthropist, lend money to this one and giving food to that one. . . . He was wont to berate me for being a usurer . . . Humph!

(*continues with the aria*)

> **Tell him to look to his bond,**
> **Tell him to look—to—his—bond!**

LEI: Why, I am sure, if he should forfeit, you will not take his flesh, will you? What's that good for?

XIA: To bait fish with. If it will feed nothing else, it will feed my revenge.

(*catching sight of* An) Humph! This is the fool that lent out money gratis.

AN: Hear me, good Master Xia—

(*sings*)

> As an old business man, I know so well
>
> You win some and you lose some—common tale.
>
> It's my ill fortune that my luck's been bad,
>
> Allow me to find some means to pay my debt.
>
> Please demonstrate your mercy generous,
>
> And grant me a reprieve of several days.

XIA: Ha! Now you call me *good* Master Xia! You used to—

(*sings*)

> Thwart bargains that I made, with efforts mad—
>
> By giving money out with open hand,
>
> Urge enemies against me, spurn me too;
>
> Laugh at my losses, hold me in disdain.
>
> If I dispute now over small details,
>
> Know that you have deserved my fullest spite!
>
> Little by little my large hatreds grew,
>
> Till time for retribution has arrived.

(*says*) Humph! You have caused me to lose many a thousand taels of shining silver! You stirred up trouble for me and

isolated me in the business world. And what's your reason?
Just because I'm a Saracen! Humph! What's really the
difference between a Saracen and a Chinese? Has not a
Saracen hands, or feet, or feelings, or passions? Is he not fed
with the same food, subject to the same diseases, as a Chinese
is?

(*sings*)

> **Likewise, we know when we feel hunger pangs;**
> **When bullied and berated, we're enraged;**
> **When sick, we too, need aid of medicine;**
> **When stabbed, we bleed and die just like you do;**
> **Ah, when can Saracens have their just day.**

(*speaks*) If I do not avenge myself on you,

(*resumes singing*)

> **Oh, how can I unload the cargo of this grief?**

AN: Master Xia—

(*sings*)

> **The times have changed,**
> **Your honor should be kind.**

(*In what follows*, Xia *and* An *sing to the same tune.*)

XIA: **I have**—(*speaks loudly*) by my god of wealth—(*resumes*
singing)

> **sworn a terrible oath,**
> **To never yield in this.**

AN: Going to court should be the last resort;
Why press it ever so relentlessly?

XIA: I'll have all done according to the bond;
When it's made up, my mind just doesn't change.

AN: My brother here has raised the needed cash;
Doubt not that I will clear the debt in full.

XIA: Are bonds to be considered trifles now?
Humph! Never doubt that I will press the suit!
(*speaks*) You used to call me dog, eh? (*gnashing his teeth*) Since I am a d—o—g, beware my fangs! Judge Bao shall grant me justice.

AN: Please, hear me speak—

XIA: I'll have my bond; I will not hear you speak. I'll have my bond; therefore speak no more. (*turns his back to him*)

BA: Fie! This fellow's a lunatic.

AN: (*despondent*) Let him alone. I'll plead to him no more. It is clear he put me in his debt on purpose. I often delivered people from his forfeitures. I know that's why he hates me.

BA: Don't worry, dear brother, I'm sure Judge Bao will support us.

(*Enter some* guards, *followed by* Judge Bao, *who takes his seat.*)

ATTENDANTS: Silence in the court!

JUDGE: (*strikes the table with a wood block*) Summon Xia Luo.

1ST GUARD: Summon Xia Luo.

(Xia Luo *steps forward and pays respects to* Judge Bao.)

JUDGE: Xia Luo—Master Xia, come forward.

The world thinks, and I think so too, that you are milking this moment for all it's worth, pretending malice to the end, but finally you'll show mercy. So although you now demand the penalty, which is a pound of this poor man's flesh, you will soon give up your claim. Moreover, touched with human gentleness and love, you will forgive a part of the principal. What has befallen him is truly so pitiable, that even the uncivilized barbarians, the stubborn Tartars, people of brassy bosoms and rough hearts of flint, would sympathize with him. And besides, this man's friend has brought the money to pay you.

BA: Yes! Here it is.

XIA: Your honor, I have already made clear my purpose; and by my god have I sworn—to have the dues for the forfeiture of my bond. If you deny it, wouldn't you be making a joke of your law?

JUDGE: Xia Luo, why would you rather choose to have a small piece of carrion flesh than to receive three thousand taels of silver?

XIA: Well—

(*sings*)

> **Enticing though the orchid's fragrance be,**
> **There are those that seek the stench of odors foul.**

> Some have a taste for stinking tofu, see,
> Some find the tender roast pig makes them howl.
> And some delight in handsome parrots' parts
> While some the pink, plump partridge do adore.
> To dress in blues and greens suits some folk's hearts,
> While some like reds and oranges so much more.
> Reasons ah, reasons there are millions, you know,
> They differ from person to person, and, so...

(*speaks*) If you keep pressing for a reason, I can give you none, except that I bear him a soul-felt hate and a relentless loathing.

(*resumes singing*)

> He's a pin in my eye, a thorn in my flesh—
> Even death is too light, his soul to enmesh!

BA: This . . . this is truly going way too far! How could you answer like this?

XIA: (*unfeelingly*) I'm not bound to please you with my answer.

BA: Do all men kill the things they do not love?

XIA: Ha! Haven't you heard of the saying "Never live under the same sky with your deadly enemy"?

AN: It would be easier to ask a tiger for its skin than argue with this Saracen. Alas, my dear brother—

(*sings*)

> Words are futile, naught but insults bear:

> **Like fools who fish the sky in fishless air.**
>
> **He, he, he pressures overbearingly**
>
> **I, I, I start to lose my wits—O, me!**
>
> **I carry all alone this deadly weight,**
>
> **Have crossed a stream of no return—too late!**

(*speaks*) Alas, there's no use wasting our breath, or trying to find any way out.   Please, your honor, sentence according to the bond and let that Saracen have his will.

BA: (*takes out banknotes*) For your three thousand taels here's six.

XIA: Were it sixty thousand, or one hundred, I would not accept it. I'll have my bond.

JUDGE: Stubborn as you are, are you not afraid of public opinion?

XIA: What judgment shall I dread, doing no wrong? The pound of flesh, which I demand of him, is dearly bought. It's mine and I will have it. Hey! Is there no enforcement of the decrees of Nisi? I stand for judgment: no more idle talk! Please, your honor, pass the sentence. Waste no more time. I have business to take care of at the stock exchange later. (*draws his knife and sharpens it on the sole of his shoe*)

JUDGE: Well . . .

BA: Why do you sharpen your knife so earnestly?

XIA: To cut the meat from that bankrupt beggar there!

BA: Not on your sole, but on your soul, do you whet your knife, oh you savage Saracen! Not even the edgy executioner's

razor-edged axe exhibits half the cutting keenness of your

sharp envy. Can no beseeching blunt this bond?

XIA: No, none that you have wit enough to make.

(*Enter* 2nd Guard.)

2ND GUARD: Your honor, a messenger from Lord Bei just arrived with

an urgent message for you.

JUDGE: Call the messenger quick.

(E*xit* 2nd Guard.)

JUDGE: For this case, we have some days ago dispatched a messenger

to the Prefecture of Duwa, entreating Lord Bei Kexin to hear

it in person.

(*Enter the messenger.*)

MESSENGER: My obeisance to your honor. At the command of

Lord Bei have I come to present an official letter.

JUDGE: Oh? Show us the letter. (*reads*) So Lord Bei has taken ill and

cannot come. He does commend Master Kuang, an assistant

of his, to hear the case on his behalf. Come, some of you, go

give Master Kuang courteous conduct to the court.

1ST GUARD: Yes, your honor. (*goes out*) Give Master Kuang

courteous conduct to the court.

MURONG: (*sings offstage*)

By clever plot have I arrived at last.—

(*Enter* Murong *and* Xingyun *disguised as men*)

MURONG: (*continues the aria*)

   It is a toil requiring craftiness.

   I've weighed the case from every angle, in

   The hope I might redeem this crisis dire.

XINGYUN: (*sings to the same tune*)

   In borrowed clothes *now thus* come I to court.

   Can anyone my gender truly spy?

MURONG: My obeisance to your honor.

JUDGE: You are Master Kuang, I presume?

MURONG: Indeed I am. And here's Mingshu, my attendant. Come, meet the lord.

(Mingshu steps forward and bows to Judge, who nods in return.)

JUDGE: Make a seat for him.

MURONG: I thank your honor.

JUDGE: Lord Bei and I are close friends. I've always been a great admirer of his scholarship and resourcefulness. Unfortunately he cannot come here in person, but he praises you profusely in the letter, commending you for your accomplishments at a tender age, and vast learning. We shall now entrust you with heavy responsibility.

MURONG: Your honor overpraises me. I'm here at your service.

JUDGE: Are you thoroughly acquainted with the present case?

MURONG: I've studied the papers, and Lord Bei has also furnished
me with his opinions.

(*faces outward*) Which is Master An here, and which the
Saracen—Xia the shop-keeper?

JUDGE: An Yibo and Xia Luo, both stand forth.

MURONG: Is your name Xia Luo?

XIA: Yes.

MURONG: This is a strange suit you bring; yet from a legal
standpoint, the law cannot impugn you for proceeding.

(*to* An) You stand within his danger, do you not?

AN: Aye, so he says.

MURONG: Do you confess the bond?

AN: I do.

MURONG: Then must the Saracen be merciful.

XIA: Why "must"? What is your reason?

MURONG: (*sings*)

The base of all humanity is mercy;

It droppeth as the gentle rain from heaven.

Good deeds are ever recompensed with good,

As witnessed truthfully in history.

The message of Liu Yi is marriage bliss.

Her bowl of rice makes rich a washerwoman.

Even beyond this life, a moment of

Commiseration can be deeply felt.

> **Be tolerant, and be magnanimous;**
>
> **Forgive where mercy seems to have a case.**
>
> **For even if your suit is just and right,**
>
> **It's well to weigh humanity with law.**
>
> **Consider both of justice and good will.**
>
> **I entreat you this: think thrice, be merciful.**

(*speaks*) I have spoken these things to mitigate the justice of your plea. If you insist on following through, I'll have to pass sentence against Master An.

XIA: My deeds upon my head! I crave the law, the penalty for the forfeit of my bond.

MURONG: Is he not able to discharge the money?

BA: Yes, I offered it to him in the court—twice the amount: if that will not suffice, I will be bound to pay it ten times over, on forfeit of my own life. If this will not suffice, it must appear that malice usurps justice. And I beseech your honor, for this once, bend the law to your authority: To do a great right, do a little wrong, and curb the will of this cruel beast.

MURONG: It must not be. The Prefect of Nisi has no power to alter an established decree. Bending it will be recorded for a precedent, resulting in many an error by the example. It cannot be.

XIA: What an upright judge! Most admirable! O wise young judge, how I do honor you!

MURONG: Please, let me see the bond.

XIA: Here it is, sir, right here.

MURONG: Master Xia, there's three times or even more silver for you.

XIA: An oath, I have an oath before the god of wealth. Shall I lay perjury upon my soul? No, not for the whole Prefecture of Nisi.

MUONG: Well, this bond is forfeit. Lawfully the Saracen may claim a pound of flesh, to be cut by him, from near the debtor's heart. Be merciful: Take thrice your money; let me tear up the bond.

XIA: Not until it is paid according to its dictates. It does appear you are a worthy judge thoroughly versed in the law. I charge you by the law, proceed with judgment. I stand by my bond.

AN: And most heartily I do beseech you to give the judgment.

MURONG: Why then—(*her eyes rolling, determined*) you must prepare your bosom for his knife.

XIA: O most just sir! Excellent!

MURONG: There is no meaning to our laws if we do not enforce their penalties, and so, I require what is due by the words of the bond.

XIA: It's very true. O wise and upright! How much more elder are you than your looks!

MURONG: Therefore lay bare your bosom.

XIA: Ay, his breast: So says the bond, does it not, noble sir?

"*Nearest—his—heart*": those are the very words.

MURONG: It is so. Is there a balance here to weigh the flesh?

XIA: I have it ready.

MURONG: Have by some surgeon, Master Xia, to stop his wounds,

lest he should bleed to death.

XIA: Is it so nominated in the bond? (*takes back the bond and*

peruses it)

MURONG: It is not so expressed, but what of that? 'Twere good you

do so much for charity.

XIA: I cannot find it; it's not in the bond.

MURONG: (*turning to* AN) As for you, Master An, have you

anything to say?

AN: Alas! But little: I am ready and am well prepared.

My dear brother—

(*sings*)

> **The fate predestined I cannot escape;**
>
> **And like a kite my life hangs by a thread.**
>
> **Our time together's now a thing of past,**
>
> **Our merry moments blown off by the wind.**
>
> **Surrounded by the dark, I laugh toward heaven,**
>
> **Content to pay for you with all my heart.**
>
> **I'll henceforth roam that undiscovered world,**
>
> **From poverty and loneliness set free.**

<blockquote>
Dear brother, grieve not that I die for you
Nor anything conceal from your sweet bride:
Our bond of brotherhood, the heavens see;
For such a bond I'll sacrifice my life.
</blockquote>

BA: (*sings*)

<blockquote>
Ah, what a sacrifice you've made for me!
There's nothing I can say through tears and shame.
Despite my deep attachment to my bride,
How can I now forget our former oath?
We met—became at once such bosom friends.
I charge the heavens with my bitter grief.
I rue my wifely journey to Beimang!
Myself I hate, that cannot die for you.
</blockquote>

(An *and* Ba *embrace each other, weeping loudly.*)

MURONG: (*sings an aside*)

<blockquote>
I thought in heaven was our marriage made,
That in his never-changing love I'd trust.
Inseparable from his sworn brother now,
He's spurned a wife to whom he promised love.
Conflicting feelings swiftly surge in me;
I must respond to this sarcastically.
</blockquote>

(*speaks*) Your wife would give you little thanks for that, if she were here.

GUA: I too have a wife, whom I dearly cherish. But now I would

she were in Western Paradise, so she could entreat Buddha to change this currish Saracen's mind.

XINGYUN: It's well you offer it behind her back—or you would be flayed alive.

XIA: We are wasting time. Please proceed to the sentencing.

MURONG: Here's my sentence. A pound of Master An's flesh is yours. The law demands it.

XIA: Most rightful sir!

MURONG: And you may cut this flesh from his breast: The law allows it.

XIA: Most learned sir! A sentence. Come! (*spit on his palms*) Let's prepare.

(*Light dims.*)

Intermission

Scene 6: The Sentence

(Location: law court of the Prefecture of Nisi)

XIA: We have wasted much of our audience's time. Please, proceed to sentence.

MURONG: Here's my sentence. A pound of Master An's flesh is yours. The court awards it, and the law does give it.

XIA: Most rightful sir!

MURONG: And you must cut this flesh from off his breast: The law allows it.

(She signals the guards, who raise An *and pull open the lapel of his robe.)*

XIA: Most learned sir! A sentence. Come, *(spit on his palms)* I'm well prepared.

(raises his knife) Come!

(hesitates a second just as he is about to stab An *in the chest. The audience in the court holds its breath and falls into dead silence.* Master Ba *covers his face in horror while* Murong *watches in cool detachment.* Xia Luo *raises his knife higher, is ready to stab)*

MURONG: One moment! There is one other thing. This bond does allow you to spill Cathayan blood. The words expressly are,

"a pound of flesh." Take then your bond, take your pound of flesh; but in cutting it, if you shed one drop of the defendant's blood, your lands and goods will be, according to existing law, confiscated by the prefecture of Nisi.

(*The crowd continues in silence for a few beats: then, they erupt in shouts of joy.*)

GUA: Oh, upright sir!

Listen to that, Saracen—ah, learned sir!

XIA: Is that the law?

MURONG: You shall see the statute yourself.

(Xia *goes forward to see.*)

For, as you urge justice, be assured you shall have justice, more than you desire.

GUA: O learned sir! Take that, Saracen: a learned sir!

XIA: I accept this offer, then; pay the bond thrice and let the Chinese go.

BA: Here is the money.

MURONG: But wait! The Saracen shall have complete justice. So wait. There is no hurry. He shall have nothing but the penalty according to the bond.

GUA: O Saracen! An upright sir, a learned sir!

MURONG: Now, go and cut off the flesh. But, shed no blood—

(*sings*)

The court has made quite clear to shed no blood.

> **Be very careful with your measurements:**
> **Be sure you cut no less nor more than this,**
> **One pound of flesh. The balance perfect be**
> **When weighed by scales. Not one ounce more or less;**
> **Not even by the weight of single hair,**
> **Or else upon my word I'll confiscate**
> **Your goods—for know well I impartial am.**

GUA: An excellent judge! A true discerning judge, Saracen! Now, you scoundrel, I have you on the hip.

MURONG: Why does the Saracen pause? Take your forfeiture.

XIA: (*drops the knife*) Give me my principal, and let me go.

BA: I have it ready for you; here it is.

MURONG: He has refused it in the open court: He shall have merely justice and the pound of flesh stipulated in the bond.

GUA: A great judge, still say I, a great judge!

XIA: Shall I not have merely my principal?

MURONG: You shall have nothing but the forfeiture, to be taken at your peril, Saracen.

XIA: (*picks up the knife, stares at it; then stares at* An, Murong, *and* Judge Bao; *slowly turns around to stare at everyone in the court; and finally sighs deeply before dropping the knife again*) Why then the devil take him! I withdraw my suit.

MURONG: Not so soon, Saracen, not so soon. The law has yet another hold on you. There is a special clause of Nisi, which

clearly states that if it be proved against an alien that by direct or indirect attempts he seeks the life of any Chinese citizen, the party he contrives against shall seize one half his goods; the other half comes to the coffer of the prefecture; and the offender's life lies at the mercy of the prefect only, against all other voices. In that predicament, I say, you now stand. For it appears, by these proceedings, that indirectly, and directly too, you have contrived against the very life of the defendant, which has been witnessed by all present in this court. Down, therefore, and beg mercy of the prefect.

GUA: Beg that you may have leave to hang yourself—and yet, your wealth being forfeit to the state, you don't even have the money to buy a cord. Well, you must be hanged at the taxpayer's expense.

JUDGE: That you may understand the Cathayan principle of forgiveness, we pardon you your life before you ask it. For half your wealth, it is Master An's; the other half comes to the treasury of the prefecture, which humbleness may turn into a fine.

XIA: Nay, take my life and all; pardon not that: you sentence me to death when you do seize my fortune.

MURONG: Master An, (Murong *signals the guards to loosen the rope around him*) what mercy can you render him?

AN: Well, I'll be content if the court reduces the government's

half into a fine, but not excuses the half due to me. Besides
this, he must immediately become a naturalized Chinese, and
he must never wear outlandish clothes anymore.

JUDGE: He shall do this, or else I will recant the pardon that I
pronounced earlier.

MURONG: Are you contented, Saracen? What do you say?

XIA: Alas—

(*sings an aside*)

> **To China's land I come from distant home,**
> **Both mountains and wild rivers have I crossed.**
> **From rags to riches, I've been scrupulous,**
> **While toiling day and night with little rest:**
> **A foreign businessman is all alone.**
> **Each year I heavy taxes surely pay;**
> **To everyone I must bow humbly down.**
> **An alien, not equal looked upon,**
> **I wept in silence when I was abused,**
> **And swallowed insults, biding still my time,**
> **Believing that the moment had arrived,**
> **And that, today, I'd finally be revenged.**
> **My knife was sharp, my stove was full of fire.**
> **How could I know that tables turn so fast,**
> **This crisp-cooked duck away flies on singed wings?**
> **Three times the principal a bargain was.**

I pushed it away; now too late for regrets.

My schemes fell sadly short of true success;

And greatest pleasure now brings greatest grief.

Wasted are my careful calculations!

A perfect written bond now binds its scribe.

What can I do, but thus embrace defeat,

Return a total bankrupt to my home.

(*speaks*) I . . . am content, I . . . have no more to say.

Your honor, I'm not well. Please give me leave to depart.

JUDGE: Get you gone.

(Xia *bows and limps out.*)

JUDGE: (*strikes the table with a wood block*) The court is dismissed. (*Exeunt all in slow motion for several seconds. Light falls on* Murong, *who shows no sign of jubilance but appears heavy-hearted.*)

JUDGE: Master Kuang, please stay. Thanks to you, this case is now satisfactorily resolved. We will have a banquet in your honor. We entreat you to stay, for there is much more that we can learn from you.

MURONG: I humbly thank your honor, but desire your honor's pardon, for I must return presently to Duwa, to see to some official business at the command of Lord Bei.

JUDGE: If that's the case, we shall not detain you. Well, please give Lord Bei my regards. I shall visit him some other time.

MURONG: Yes, your servant shall tell him so.

JUDGE: (*turns to* An) Master An, you must thank Master Kuang for his help.

AN: Yes, yes, your honor.

(*Exeunt.*)

Scene 7: Offering Thanks

(Location: Nisi, outside of the law court)

BA: Most worthy gentleman, by your wisdom my friend has been this day spared his life. (*takes out banknotes*) The three thousand taels of silver, due unto the Saracen, we freely offer to you as a small token of appreciation. Please do accept it.

AN: Indeed I stand indebted, over and above, in love and service to you evermore.

MURONG: My mind was never yet mercenary. That I had this opportunity to deliver you from bad luck must have been preordained. As long as the case is satisfactorily concluded I am content. It's a small thing unworthy of mentioning. (*pauses; to Ba, meaningfully*) I pray you, know me when we meet again: I wish you both well, and so I take my leave.

BA: Well, dear sir, pardon my boldness, but do take some remembrance of us, as a tribute, not as a fee.

MURONG: (*hesitates for a second*) You press me far, therefore I must yield.
(*pointing at Ba's finger*) That ring—may I have it as a remembrance?

BA: This ring? (*hesitates, drawing back his hand*) Alas, it is a

trifle! . . . I will not shame myself to give you this.

MURONG: Really? I rather like its color and translucence, very suggestive of a gentleman. Let me have this ring then.

BA: This is not an expensive ring, but there's more that depends on this ring than its price, so I can't part with it. If you don't mind, I'll purchase a dearer ring for you. (*looking at the ring*) Only for this, I beg your pardon.

MURONG: Oh I see, sir, you are liberal in offers. You teach me first how to beg, and then you teach me how a beggar should be answered.

BA: No, no, no, good sir, you're mistaken. This ring was given me by my wife; and I made a vow that it would never part from my hand.

MURONG: That's a good excuse for saving gifts. If your wife is reasonable, she would know how well I have deserved the ring. I take my leave.

(Murong *pretends to be contemptuous, then turns to* Xingyun, *sniggering and nodding knowingly. They exit.*)

AN: My dear brother, let him have the ring: he saved my life!

BA: Well . . .

AN: (*sings*)

> **Since you departed seeking fortune fair,**
>
> **I tried to cheerful look, but gained no peace.**
>
> **My ships were wrecked and nowhere to be found**

While to my great alarm, bond was required.

I tried for loans from all, but no success;

Walled in by grief, I watched my hair turn gray.

And only taunts from creditor I heard.

My neck was in the rope, and all was lost.

By terrifying dreams, I haunted was,

Night after night from dusk to break of day,

My mind, like surging well, filled with distress;

The torture seemed to be without an end.

In deep despair I was resolved to die,

When unexpectedly I then was saved!

For sure the jade ring signifies an oath,

Yet still, it's a piece of rock—no more.

But rescuing a life's a favor large!

(*speaks*) My dear brother, it is *my life* that he saved!

(*resumes singing*)

And does this not outweigh—mere vow to maid?

BA: (*sings*)

The things he's saying do seem sensible.

I should've given it without a thought.

(*raises his hand, but stops in the act of taking off the ring*)

(*sings an aside*)

What if my lady does not understand,

But takes offense and therefore won't forgive?

(*pondering, aside*) What shall I do?

(Chorus, *offstage*):

> **He is my brother dear, steadfast and true;**
>
> **She is my lady dear, faithful and fair.**
>
> **To give this ring or no?—I puzzled am.**
>
> **How to decide? My dull, dual mind's in duel.**

AN: (*hurrying him*) Dear brother, quickly send the ring to Master Kuang, before he is out of reach.

BA: Well . . .

(*looks at the ring, then at An; repeats these actions; tormented*)

AN: My dear brother . . .

BA: (*finally making up his mind*) Well, then.

(*resumes singing*)

> **How can all things turn out as we might wish?**
>
> **Better, on time, repay great debts of thanks.**

(*taking off the ring, speaks*) Go, Gua Nuo, run and overtake Master Kuang and give him the ring.

(*Light dims.*)

Scene 8: The Bargain

(*Location: the reception room of the Murong mansion in Beimang County*)

MURONG: (*sings*)

Now all I hear is noise of wind and rain:

How dreary, desolate is this deep night!

In my heart, fits of pain unfit for words:

His thoughtlessness alone is what's to blame.

Forgotten are his solemn oaths of love,

My earnest words and wishes at his pledge.

What can true love say to the faithless now?

So sorrow-filled, I know not what to do.

(*staring at the ring in her hand*)

(*speaks*) This is truly unbelievable. . . . I thought . . . and yet he . . . so carelessly . . .

(*Enter* Xingyun *with a tea tray.*)

XINGYUN: Indeed, madam. I can' believe that Gua Nuo, that minion, should follow the example of my lord. Just some chitchat, and he gave that attendant the ring I had given him as a token of love. (*stomps her foot*) How it annoys me!

MURONG: When they return, Xingyun, we will settle this!

(*Enter the* Steward.)

STEWARD: Madam, my lord and his friends are returned.

MURONG: Say I shall greet them outside.

STEWARD: (*announces*) My lady will greet them outside.

(Murong *and* Xingyun *go out as* Ba, An, Gua *enter. They greet each other and go into the reception room.*)

MURONG: Welcome back, my lord.

BA: I thank you, madam.

Ah, allow me to introduce a bosom friend. Come, this is the man, this is Master An—my dear brother, to whom I am so infinitely bound.

MURONG: (*salutes gracefully*) My respects to you, Brother An! Welcome to our house. Your favor, as I've heard, is indeed so great it is hard to reciprocate.

(Xingyun *leads* Gua *away by the hand; they whisper to each other.*)

AN: (*returns the salute*) Don't mention it!

BA: Fortunately everything's alright now.

GUA: (*to* Xingyun, *loudly*) By heaven I swear you do me wrong! In faith, I gave it to Master Kuang's attendant. See how you storm!

MURONG: What's the matter, Xingyun? A quarrel, now? In front of

a guest? Shame on you.

BA: That's alright. Brother An is no stranger.

AN: No, no, I'm no stranger. Please consider me one of the family.

MURONG: Well, then, Gua Nuo, you speak first.

GUA: Madam, it's about a hoop of gold, a paltry ring that she did give me, whose posy was for all the world like cutler's poetry upon a knife.

XINGYUN: Do you remember what it was?

GUA: Sure. It was nothing but "Love me, and leave me not."

XINGYUN: Ha! How amazing you should still remember it!

(*sings*)

> **Talk you of "Love me, and leave me not"?**
> **How little is the value of these words!**
> **You were the man who swore an oath to me**
> **That you would wear it till the day you died.**
> **But look: how soon you lapsed to faithlessness.**
> **What insolence to fuss with such a noise**
> **When you've gone out and found another love!**
> **Confess; don't try to trick with false excuse.**
> **Look in your soul and see there who's at fault.**
> **'Tis fair or not?—Let Heaven be my judge!**

GUA: Now, by this hand, I gave it to a youth, Master Kuang's attendant. A little scrubbed boy—hmm, no taller than yourself. A prating boy; he begged it as a fee. I could not for my heart

deny it him.

MURONG: It is your fault then, Gua Nuo. How could you part so slightly with your wife's token of love. Besides, you'd sworn to cherish it forever. No wonder Xingyun is so mad. I should have been furious.

BA: (*aside*) Why, I had better cut this finger off and swear I lost it defending the ring.

GUA: My lord also gave his ring away, to Master Kuang, who indeed deserved it too; and then the boy, his attendant, who followed him around, he begged mine. And neither man nor master would take anything but the two rings. What else could I do?

MURONG: Oh? What ring did you give him, my lord? Not that, I hope, which you received from me.

BA: Well, to be honest, it was that one. I too did it against my will.

MURONG: Against your will? Humph! (*flicks her sleeve in anger*)

BA: Cease your anger, madam, and listen to me.
Alas! If you did know to whom I gave the ring, for whom I gave the ring, for what I gave the ring, and how unwillingly I gave the ring, you would surely not be so violently displeased.

MURONG: Humph! If you had known the virtue of the ring, or her worthiness that gave the ring, or how you should cherish the ring, you would not then have parted so lightly with the ring.

BA: Ah, my dear lady—

(*sings*)

> Dangers lurked on all sides that court day;
>
> I argued fiercely, not to be outdone.
>
> Severity in law should tempered be;
>
> That Saracen! That cur, a heart of flint!
>
> A paper would have cost my brother's life
>
> But for the intervening Master Kuang.
>
> I offered in my thanks, three thousand taels,
>
> Yet, he'd have nothing—but the ring of jade.
>
> Reluctant, hesitant was I; I weighed
>
> My choices but could not make up my mind.
>
> I'm so indebted to good An's dear care,
>
> Nor earth nor sky forgives ingratitude!

(*speaks*) Madam, truly I felt I had no choice but to give the ring.

MURANG: (*sings*)

> That jade, the token of my love, is naught;
>
> A husband's oath it seems is worth still less.
>
> "I'll follow you until my life does end"—
>
> Those are the very words you spoke to me.
>
> Now rashly have you cast the ring aside;
>
> Perhaps you've found another lovely girl?
>
> Perhaps you have two faces? Your love's changed?
>
> Perhaps your ardor's drifting like frail smoke?

> Perhaps love's like a dream you can't recall?
> World's ruled by withered flowers, waning moon?
> Our love as man and wife is at an end;
> Why then should I care so much for—*that ring!*

GUA: (*bursts into laughter at the bawdy pun*) Ha, that ring! *That— ring!*

BA: (*stares at him*) Is this the time for mirth?

MURONG: (*her eyes rolling, speaks*) Why would a normal man ask for such a thing from you? That person must be a woman!

BA: No, by my honor, madam, it wasn't a woman. Had you been there, I'm sure you would have begged the ring of me to give Master Kuang.

MURONG: Well, well, well! Since you've given him the jade ring, you might as well send me to him!

XINGYUN: That's right, send me as a gift to his attendant. I'd be happy to share my bed with him!

GUA: (*furious*) Humph! Let me not see him, then; if I do—I'll geld him!

AN :   Ah, well, I am the unhappy subject of these quarrels . . .

MURONG: Never mind, sir; you are our guest of honor.

BA: Pardon this fault, my dear wife, and I swear I will never do it again. (*bows low to her*) Do accept my apologies.

MURONG: Did you hear that? He just made another oath . . .

BA: Well, madam, (*kneels to make a vow*) Heaven and earth be

my witness: I, Ba Wuji, hereby swear never to disappoint my lady. If I should violate this oath, may I be struck dead by thunderbolt!

AN: Well, madam, I once did lend a pound of my body for his wealth, which almost cost my life. Now I dare be bound again, my body upon the forfeit, that your lord will never more break faith.

MURONG: Then you shall be his surety. (*produces the jade ring*) Give him this, and bid him keep it better than the other.

AN: My dear brother, (*passes to him the ring*) this time you should take extra care.

BA: Certainly, most certainly! As long as I can breathe, this ring shall never part from me . . . (*examines the ring*)

(Xingyun *also produces the gold ring and gives it to* Gua.)

XINGYUN: You, too, must take good care of it.

BA: Look, it is the same I gave Master Kuang!

MURONG: Of course! It was the token of love that Master Kuang gave me.

XINGYUN: My dear Gua Nuo, this was given me by that scrubbed attendant.

GUA: What? Then there's a pair of cuckolds, you and me.

MURONG: Speak not so grossly.

(*proudly*) You are all amazed. See, here is a letter, from my cousin—Lord Bei, Prefect of Duwa. Read it and you shall

find that I was Master Kuang, Xingyun my attendant.

(*All the others on stage are dumbstruck.*)

AN: Unbelievable!

BA: (*sizing her up*) Were you Master Kuang and I knew you not?

GUA: Were you the attendant that is to make me cuckold?

XINGYUN: That's me!

BA: Ha ha ha . . . My dear wife, (*bows*) Master Kuang, we rushed
our marriage ceremony last time. Shall we do it all over again?

(Murong *looks askance at him, not exactly smiling, and appears
nonchalant.* Ba *steps forward in an attempt to cuddle* Murong, *who
turns slightly away from him;* Gua *cuddles* Xingyun. *The two pairs
exit, leaving An on stage alone, dejected and despondent.*)

AN: (*sings*)

Bygones are bygones: no use looking back.

These marriages are real, have clearly come.

To whom now do I show my loyal heart?

I've no one left; it's all come to an end.

A bond as strong as stone has just dissolved.

I would be drunk on wine to dull this grief!

(*Light dims.*)

Epilogue

(The wedding ceremony, observed by Master An *etc. Enter* Master Ba *and* Murong, *followed by* Gua Nuo *and* Xingyun. *They perform the rites by first bowing to Heaven and Earth, but, when it's time for the bridegroom and the bride to bow to each other,* Murong *stands straight. Freeze.)*

(Chorus, *offstage*):

> **New lyrics penned in classic formulation,**
> **Bond hopes to offer food for meditation.**
> **If close relationships must come to end,**
> **Where can one find on earth a bosom friend?**
> **However fair and square the law may be,**
> **One need not press it too insistently.**
> **Blind passion only leads to endless rue;**
> **The moon alone can Heaven's will construe.**

The End